Everything at Christmas C
Emma Jordan

License Notes
All rights reserved. No part of this book may be reproduced in any form without written permission from the author. Reviewers may quote brief passages in reviews.
This book is licensed for your personal enjoyment only. This book may not be resold or given away to other people. If you would like to share this book with another person, please purchase an additional copy for each recipient. If you're reading this book and did not purchase it, or it was not purchased for your use only, then please purchase your own copy. Thank you for respecting the hard work of this author.

For Eve, still always my favourite reader and writer.

Week Four

1st – 7th December

Elle

A pelican swoops down in front of me, beak first, breaking into the water.

I love watching these huge, graceful birds biding their time on a palm branch, which really doesn't seem strong enough to hold their ungainly frame, before they glide and dive swiftly, without hesitation, into the ocean to catch dinner. They know what they want and they're successful.

I reach for my drinks bottle on the table and sip the warming water, as I watch the wingspan of these magnificent birds dart to my left, between the green fronds and orange sky. I'll never tire of sunsets by the sea, but tonight there is no canvas propped up in front of me.

Jam and I have only been in Belize for a couple of weeks, taking a holiday from our working holiday. We spent the autumn with Cassie, just outside Ecuador's capital, Quito, teaching art and music to the children at the school she works with, while she managed her latest project of building a new school in the highlands of the Andes. I loved being in the mountains and what definitely felt like the centre of the world. The altitude sickness that comes with spending time almost 3000m above sea level was certainly a new experience. Slight headaches and a little dizziness. Not too dissimilar to some hangovers I've had. Sipping coffee slowly once or twice a day hadn't been too bad either. I could live without the humidity, with no cool water to escape into, apart from the hotel pools, despite the country have some of the best Pacific coast.

Next week Jam and I fly out to Bankgok and then onto the Thai island we spent last Christmas on; our first Christmas together.

Rather like the big-beaked bird in front of me, I'm following the sun, east instead of south. I could get used to the life of a perpetual wanderer, living remotely. Nomadic people have always moved to where the work is, and where their soul needs to be free. We're no different in the 21st century.

Christmas is on the horizon, though. The season should be a time for family, but I've never had a family Christmas. Maybe I just feel guilty for not spending time with Lucy? They'll be in Cornwall this year, anyway.

Last year, we'd been living in Thailand, on the beach, spending the day with friends, although I didn't remain in touch with anyone. Being around people I didn't mind had been a welcome change from the loneliness I had normally felt over the holidays, working and studying.

And Jam had been right there with me on Christmas Day, though he's since shared that he usually went hiking, alone, for the three days of the holidays.

Each time I'd glanced over at him last Christmas, he looked like he'd been watching me. I hadn't realised how he'd felt about me then, or the depth of my own feelings for him. It had been the following day, Boxing Day, when I'd opened up my heart to James.

And wherever we were, I always wanted to be with him.

How could I tell him that I wanted to spend Christmas with Lucy and her family, just because I was beginning to appreciate them, when he'd lost his parents to the Boxing Day Tsunami at age 12? No, I'd settle for a February New Year celebration in Nashville; maybe they could have a smaller, second Christmas instead of Valentine's? I'm sure my nieces would love that idea.

I stare out towards the sun sinking over the dock, wondering how I would paint this sunset. It didn't matter that I had a book of sunsets from the last few months; each passing of day into darkness was unique. I'd started playing around with creating prints, which are a lot more portable than the canvases I work on when we're in England's surf capital, Newquay, or on Cornwall's western Lizard Peninsula.

Just before the sun drops below the horizon, I see Jam walk towards me, fresh from his chat with the hotel's host about a group dive at the barrier reef.

My man reaches down to kiss me, our foreheads connecting, breathing each other in - as if it had been more than half an hour since we'd seen each other. He always has time for more than a quick peck on the lips that so many of my former boyfriends considered a suitable welcome. I answer his energy with my own, before remembering we're still on a public beach. We draw apart and he sinks down onto the chair next to me, his hand reaching out for mine, keeping our skin connected. I had never needed to be so close to a man all the time. He was everything to me; we had a lifetime of Christmases together.

'All set for the dive tomorrow.' He said, outlining the trip with guests from a nearby island. All I had to know was what time we were due on the boat, and to make sure we were awake a good hour before.

As I said, I needed to be close to this man as much as possible, and he is equally obsessed. The last three months we've been together have proved that.

Lucy

For the last hour sleep has been taunting me.

Cain, curled up on the edge of the bed, is snoring as rhythmically as a musician can. My mind is travelling in circles, to or from an anonymous destination I'm not sure. Em will be awake soon, which defers sleep even more.

It's been three nights that Emily's been unsettled now, refusing to go to sleep or stay asleep until she drops.

Cain and I have taken it in turns to try to sooth her, while the other one of us sleeps. She must be so excited about her first visit from Santa in a few weeks. Or, more likely, the change in weather and additional people we've had over for Thanksgiving has hindered her routine more than we'd thought.

Still, a baby is able to learn or unlearn something in just a few days, so I'm hopeful we've ridden out the worst of the sleepless nights, ahead of our trip to the UK for Christmas.

She cries out, a piercing, demanding, yell, and Cain pulls back the covers to attend to her. I lay a hand on his shoulder.

'It's okay, darling, I'll see to her; you have those interviews in the morning – well, in just a few hours.'

He nods, reaching over to share a kiss, his warm breath on my lips too brief; he's asleep before his head hits the pillow. I smile as I hurry out to see Emily before she wakes Lottie. Although, our eldest sleeps as heavily as her Dad.

Emily's smile quickly reaches her huge blue eyes when she sees me. There's a reason babies are so adorable. Although, at nine months she's not so tiny anymore. I try to lull her back to sleep, suggesting in a soothing voice that three in the morning isn't the right time to wake up.

I warm a small bottle of milk for Em, which she guzzles, but there is no sign of sleep in her wide smile. I carry her downstairs, switching on the coffee pot and wandering into the living room to switch on the TV for us.

A few daft cartoons later and we were both asleep on the sofa in minutes, my coffee growing cold on the side table. My last thought was how we were going to handle the flight to England next month without a sofa and a coffee machine.

I open my eyes to find Cain rocking Em in his arms, and Lottie watching her energetic cartoons. He reaches down to kiss me awake, whispering those sexy words, 'fresh coffee and pancakes in the kitchen'. The man still knows how to make my knees weak after over five years together. And while he drives half the country-music-buying population crazy with weakness, too, he's a family man, just like his brother, just like their dad, and home is where his heart is.

We would make Christmas in Cornwall work, somehow; I'd find lots of activities to keep Em occupied, and I know I won't be solely responsible for calming her vocal communications.

Nancy

Joe has just driven last night's guest to the railway station, and I'm taking advantage of a quiet day free of any visitors to the guest house to update my Christmas notes before Cassie, Jason, Cain and their families come home to Cornwall for Christmas.

A large, freshly brewed cup of tea sits on the table in front of me, and I'm tucked up on the sofa. I check the food order first. I ordered the meat in October, but I want to make sure I'll have the right sized turkey, ham and beef from the butcher, for Christmas Day, then the steaks for Christmas Eve need to be added to the list, along with our regular pie and meat order. There can never be enough bacon in the house when family comes to visit.

I place a tick near the list and sip my tea. I feel like a new mum enjoying a hot drink for the first time. I'm often distracted by guests admiring the view over the Atlantic Ocean, or asking about boat tours nearby, or rainy day activities. I'm always happy to help, of course, but it does mean tea is often lukewarm.

Next, book the coastal Santa Express trains for Charlotte and Emily, although I suspect that Ben and Olivia will still want to see Santa, too, despite their teen years; there's always a gift and a hot chocolate as well as the lights along the coast to enjoy – although even their Dads still enjoy the magical experience, too, possibly something to do with the hot mulled wine available for grown-ups.

Then there's the room organisation.

A baby takes up so much more space than their physical selves, with travel cots and high chairs and booster seats, not to mention nappy changing space. But this is going to be my newest granddaughter's first Christmas here on the Cornish coast, so Lucy and Cain will have the largest room in the guest house. Jason and Shelly will be across the hall, so they can have a little quiet time. Cassie will have her room back, the one Elle stayed at the start of the year. Olivia will share with Lottie, as Ben, an older teenager now, needs his own space. Jason and Cain won't give him or Olivia any room to breathe during the day, with the coves being so close by and wild swimming running through the veins of their uncle. I shudder at the thought of the icy temperatures.

There. Done. For now.

I drop the book next to me on the sofa and finish the rest of my tea.

It doesn't feel like there's a free minute from the August Bank Holiday to December, when the guest house is full of visitors from further afield in Cornwall and nearby Devon, enjoying the most of the good autumnal weather.

Once the last guest has departed and the rooms are cleaned, they'll be aired out. Joe and I had a week off in October, visiting Jason and Shelly up in Cheshire. Then it's back to business; the family business of Christmas.

I absolutely love having everyone together, and we've been lucky enough to have a summer holiday in California this year, so we were all together for a week. But Christmas is the time to go overboard with love. Even Cassie is coming back home from South America for a week. It's a shame Lucy's sister Elle and Jam won't be around, spending their Christmas out in Thailand, but they'll find their way to Cornwall soon enough when the UK waters warm up again.

I take my cup into the kitchen and warm up the oven for our lunchtime steak pasties. This afternoon Joe can retrieve the decorations from the loft so we'll see what needs replacing. We always have two trees at Christmas, one in the hallway entrance, and the main tree in the living room, and I want to make sure we have enough lights to go around the bedrooms. We only replaced our outside lights a couple of years ago so I'll ask Mr Davies' teenage son, Max, to set up the outside decorations. Our job now is to supervise the grunt work.

Cassie

My feet pound the pavement in their familiar way as the thought-on-a-loop beats its own rhythm to my Abba playlist - why on earth did I tell Mum I'd be able to make it home for Christmas this year? Why, why?

Even though it is only a week I've planned off, literally arriving in the UK on the 23rd December and being back in Ecuador for the New Year, I have no idea how I'm going to finish the build of the school before my supposed flight, which I have yet to book.

Still, Christmas is four weeks away, and I have no partner requiring me to be home by a certain time, so working 14-hour days combining teaching duties with overseeing the building project should work, before I fly home. I want the younger children to be able to go to their new school in the new year, hopefully January, and have their fighting chance of an education, for however brief a time, before work and earning money for the family calls them away.

This project is why I spent six months in China, earning enough money in half the time, to reinvest in my dream of building a new school in the poorest area of Quito. All those Asian meetings I held, late into the night in karaoke bars, belting out Ed Sheeran tracks, securing investment for the vision I created, cannot all have been for nothing. I'll dig down deep and find the physical resources I now need. I've always relied on myself, I will do again.

I round the corner to my block to finish up my 10k run and bound up the stairs to my apartment. A quick shower, breakfast and then I'll walk the twenty minutes to class, teaching children aged 6 - 10 until their lunch break and end of the school day. Then I'll check in on the construction and nip back to the office for a quick sandwich at my desk while I continue with teacher recruitment for January. I need teachers who have spent at least two years in South America, to be fluent in the culture as well as the language.

If I repeat this routine every day, maybe Christmas will become the furthest thing from my mind, as will plans for next year when the school is running smoothly. Maybe I'll stay, maybe I'll need to head to the Middle East for my next teaching role and take advantage of the tax breaks? Perhaps I could head to a cooler country - Switzerland? I've been teaching around the world for over ten years now, and travelling during the summer months. My next three years look vaguer than they ever have done.

   I'm so glad my social life is quiet right now.

Week Three

8th - 14th December

Lucy

I just need Em to have her afternoon nap, then I can go sort out the suitcases we need to take to England.

But Em has other ideas – life has suddenly become very intriguing and she's crawling around, absolutely refusing to sleep. This house is normally so full of people, yet everyone has managed to find a task to do, so they don't have to deal with an active baby. Thank goodness Lottie is in playgroup so I only have to occupy one child.

'Oh, I know you're learning, sweetie. But Mummy has lots and lots of jobs to do, if we're to leave the country on time.' I sing, thinking of the rapidly growing list in my pocket-sized notebook.

I don't want to think about the series of flights and car journeys. Or how much stuff children need to take with them, AND then there's the clothes, and the gifts.

Em looks up from her position on the play mat and gurgles, her big blue eyes already planning mischief. I crouch down to her, to see what's caught her interest. The necklace Cain bought me for my last birthday; the diamond has definitely focussed her eyes. She's going to love her first Christmas, with all the twinkly lights and sparkly people. She thumps her favourite teddy on the floor and I smile at her.

Looks like I'm not packing today.

I roll a toy towards her, laughing as she follows its movement, then turns over as she makes up her mind to go after the little wooden car. Maybe the more active she is in the day time, the more she'll sleep through the night?

Not a chance.

I certainly don't remember Lottie being this active in her first year. She used to just lie there and whack whatever came into view. She was always content to watch, but was happiest sat with books and toys or watching TV; like mother, like daughter, that one. Em certainly takes after Cain's adventurous side.

'Hello, beautiful girls.' Cain announces. Em's head turns immediately towards him and her teddy is whacked even harder on the floor. He drops his bag on the floor and drops down to play with us, wrapping me up in a hug, his lips lingering on mine for a few heartbeats.   Then he's play-chasing Em and she's squealing with pure happiness.

I want to tackle the million jobs I have to do, but I also want to stay here with my family. I really, really do.

But dinner plans, and laundry and chasing up tasks on the To Do list.

I reluctantly stand, my hand resting on Cain's shoulders.

'I'm off to start the packing for England. Then I'll go and pick Lottie up. Are you okay to do dinner?'

'Sure. Em and I will cook up a storm in the kitchen. Are you ready for steak yet?'

She laughs like she's already developing her own brand of sass.

The last time we travelled was a trip to Chicago in May. All we had to do was load up the car and Cain drove the few hours north. It was an adventure.

The thought of repeating that journey to get to an airport, for a nine hour flight, with such an active – and vocal – little one, and then the six hour drive west to Cornwall...?

I shudder.

But, the flights are booked, Nancy has ordered tons of food, the guest house is wildly decorated, Jase and Shelly will be heading over a couple of days after we've arrived.

I sink onto the bed, taking deep breaths in through my nose, out through my mouth, trying to regain a sense of where I am; I'm not yet in a car or on a plane.

Everything is okay. I'm okay.

I close my eyes, and look for my blue.

Cain's eyes. He'll be with me. We're doing this journey together. His reserves of energy can handle Em. I'll sit with Lottie and watch films. It'll be okay.

But why do I feel it won't?

I take a few further deep breaths, filling my lungs with hope as much as controlled air. But I still feel claustrophobic. I take out my phone from my jeans pocket and dial Elle, wandering into my closet. I loved sharing this space with her when she visited so much in the spring. I haven't seen her in months, and I miss my sister.

She picks up quickly, as if her phone was in her hand. Which it always is.

'Hey, Sis.'

'It sounds noisy, where are you?'

'Airport. We've been waiting ages for a connecting flight, after our earlier one to London was delayed. Jam says Hi. Luce?'

I'd forgotten about delays. About airport security. About trying to placate a baby in a crowded place with lots of germs and strangers and nowhere for them to play or sleep.

'Luce?' Elle repeats.

'I can't do it.'

'Can't do what? Where are you?'

'In the closet.'

'Ohh, your closet. Bigger than our last apartment in Belize. Although we did overlook the Caribbean Sea. Your home is amazing.'

'I know; I don't want to leave. I feel like I'm in a snow globe that people can't stop shaking. One of those old fashioned ones from a department store, right by the front entrance.'

'What are you talking about, Sis? Is everything okay? Where's Cain?'

'We're all good.' I sigh, remembering how worried she'd been about us, just after Em had been born, when I struggled with being a Mum to two and a wife to one of the most in-demand musicians of his time. I know that Cain is such a family man, now only touring for a few weeks at a time, instead of all-year round; he loves home as much as I do.

'I can't travel to England.'

'When? Oh, for Christmas!'

'I want Em's first Christmas to be at home. Not scarred by travelling halfway around the world with a terrified Mum who shrieks and hollers. I know babies travel, and I know I'm not on my own trying to do this. And I know we have flights booked, but the thought of leaving Nashville makes me kind of wobble, you know.'

'So don't go. What does Cain think?'

'I don't know - I've sort of just vocalised my thoughts out loud now. There's a reason I've been putting off the packing, though.'

'Cain will be absolutely fine with whatever you need. Oh, they're calling our flight – at last – got to go. Let me know how everything goes. Think we have a few random hours in London then we're off to Bangkok.'

'I will do. Thanks, Elle. Give Jam a huge squeeze from me.'

'No problems. Love you, Sis.'

She rings off, but I don't move from the chair in my closet. It's so quiet in here. I tap the snow globe app on my phone and shake it gently, watching the snow scatter. I love this about technology. Despite it reflecting how I've been feeling, it's oddly relaxing; I can be in control of the chaos, right?

I'm just thinking about moving when I hear footsteps. Cain and Em peep around the doorframe. Cain's smile shifts when he sees me slumped on the oversized chair, still clutching my phone.

'Luce?' He crouches down, level to my face.

I look up into his ocean-coloured eyes, lay my head on that wonderful spot between his head and shoulder, and take several deep breaths. His free arm wraps around me. Em gurgles away, her tiny fingers clutching onto my hair.

'I don't want to go back to England for Christmas.' I exhale.

'How come?'

'The thought of all that travelling. And being away from Em's home on her first Christmas, her bed and her toys.'

'Okay.'

'Okay?'

'I'll let Mum know tonight, we'll exchange our flights.'

'What?' I sit up and see the acceptance in his face. Just like that.

'I don't care where we are, as long as we're all together, and always are.'

'Cain Adams, you are pretty perfect, you know?'

'I do, but I'm always happy to be reminded.'

He reaches across to kiss me, his mouth fitting so gorgeously to mine.

Em tugs our hair, pulling us apart, and I reach down to cuddle our youngest daughter for a few minutes, before I head out to pick up our eldest. I send Elle a quick message to let her know that we'll be celebrating Christmas in Nashville.

I hope Nancy is okay with the new plans. But I can't deny that suddenly I feel lighter, like the snow has settled in the snow globe of my mind.

Elle

After speaking with Lucy, who I had to admit had me a little worried, I can't shake a negative feeling from my mind. I've seen the opening and closing credits to two films, but I couldn't tell you what happened on the miniature screen in front of me.

Jam's sleeping in his airline bed, his long legs still, the duvet pulled up to his chin. He always gets cold on flights. I stand up to stretch my legs, smiling at the flight attendant. We're the only two people in First today; travelling halfway around the world on a random midweek day in early December apparently isn't popular for a lot of people.

I lean down to tuck Jam's duvet down over his exposed back, and he stirs awake.

'Sssh.' Go back to sleep.' I hush. 'We're still only halfway across the Atlantic.'

'Hmmm, my favourite place to be with you.'

'In it,' I grin.

He hauls up the duvet and pulls me down towards him, laying me on top of him, and wrapping us together.

'Health and safety and all that?'

'I got you, Elle. And the seat belt sign is off, so we're good.'

I can't resist a quick cuddle with my man, his body feeling just right under mine. A year ago we'd just arrived in Thailand together for the first time. I had no idea of the anguish he was about to go through, again, nor that I'd finally realise how important he was to become to me.

I'm right at home wherever he is.

Returning to Thailand has delivered a flood of memories to my senses, some of them very welcome.

As last time, we kept our time in Bangkok at a minimum, just enough time to recharge in a hotel, and enjoy a vast array of street food. I was still the number one fan of Chicken Pad Thai, with the delicious lime and peanut flavours. The next morning we flew on a domestic flight to the airport nearest the southern Thai island, and a boat to the place we'd call home for the next month. Christmas on a beach was everyone's idea of paradise, right? How could I be with the man I loved and still want more?

We were due to visit Nashville in February, but perhaps I could persuade Jam to head over for a second Christmas with Lucy?

Malee and Don approach the sand as the boat pulls up, waving excitedly to us. Malee waves her younger brother out to help us with luggage. She watches us, her long straight black hair smooth over her shoulder, a warm smile on her face.

'Wah, you're so strong now Don! It's all the drumming you've been doing?' Jam asks, high-fiving him as he jumps off the boat.

'Football, basketball, running; it's all the sports!' He yells.

As soon as she reaches me Malee swoops in to hug me.

'Sawadikap; welcome back, Elle. We missed you.'

'I'm sorry I left so suddenly.'

Her smile broadens. 'No need to be sad, your heart had to do what your heart had to do. I am so happy for you and for Jam.'

'Did I hear my name?' Jam reaches down to hug the woman who has been his friend for almost two decades, who had lost her sister in the Boxing Day Tsunami.
They walk us to the nearby lodge that we're staying in.

'There are no expat teachers like last year' Malee says. 'We have plenty of tourists, who are responsible and help us to look after the land, cleaning the beaches. And they don't travel to that movie island. The teachers we have now are older and have brought their families. I run a cooking school now, for our guests. Elle, I will teach you how to make your favourite. I'll give you good price on lessons.' She smiles, flicking her hair behind her shoulder.

I could probably live off a diet of Pad Thai pretty happily.

After Jam and I unpack and refresh, change into long sleeves and long trousers, we head out to the evening sunset. Malee has reserved a rattan four poster bed on the beach for us and set up a table for dinner to enjoy our first night back in Thailand. The cream, cotton side drapes are down, for privacy, but we've left the front rolled up, to watch the sun sparkle on the water.

'I can't believe how so much has changed over the last year.' Jam says, reaching for my hand.

I thread the fingers of my left hand through his, sipping the iced coffee that I have definitely missed as I lean into him.

'But I know that I'm not dreading the 26th December, as I normally would, because you're here with me. Last year I'd grown used to your distractions, we all ate together so often. But I had thought the day would be the necessary pain of remembering that it always has been painful. And then I saw you. I really saw you. You'd not been Lucy's annoying kid sister for a while, but I hadn't allowed myself to think of you as a beautiful butterfly, fluttering around everyone, making a social community for us.'

'Jam.' I falter.

'I don't mean that in a bad way. You created a wonderful atmosphere around us all last year. I'd thought you were a bit of a diva, but I loved getting to know you.'

'And then I left.' I said, sadly.

'It was a confusing time, for both of us.' He raises our hands, places delicate kisses on my knuckles, clutches me to his chest, then he grins at me. 'I don't think I told you that Alex tried it on with me, after you left.'

'The cheeky mare!' I laugh, remembering the secret excursions she used to take with one of the other teachers. 'To be fair, she had suggested you were next on her list.'

'Don't worry, I didn't.'

'I know. You'd have told me before now.'

'I would.'

Then we turn towards each other, the sun and dinner momentarily forgotten.

'Knock, knock.' Malee sings as she approaches. I sit up first and head for the table, followed by Jam.

She places the deliciously fragrant food before us; Jam's favourite Pad Kaphrao, a rice dish with fish sauce, basil and seafood and my prawn Pad Thai, flavoured with lime and peanut, on a plate. There's a beer for Jam and my favourite iced coffee.

'Khawp jai.' Jam says, clasping his hands together, and bowing. I repeat my thanks.

Malee leaves us, smiling, and we admire our delicious meals. I squeeze the lime halves over my dinner, inhaling the aroma, before picking up my chopsticks. Jam lifts his fork and starts to work on his rice. The silence is comforting.

'Imagine lots of these dishes for Christmas Day?' Jam suddenly announces, leaning back into his chair, happiness written all across his face and an empty bowl in front of him. 'This is going to be the best Christmas I've had in years.'

I continue to chew the last of my prawns, moving the noodles to one side. The sinking feeling has returned to my stomach. It's not the food. Perhaps tiredness is catching up with me?

Cassie

The sun rises on a new day in the school yard in Quito.

I've been in class for an hour, setting the vocabulary up on the board for the children to learn and going through the recent book donations we've received. There's a good selection today, from a vintage bookstore I've used since September. Readers donate to an account at the store and when fifty books can be paid for, they're mailed to me. I had to explain that I was looking for a mix of English language and Spanish language books, to support reading in school and for pleasure. Today's haul is twenty-five of each. I leaf through the familiar picture books that will be great for our younger learners. There are several stories about football and a few about fairies. A few earlier versions of Harry Potter have also been sent. With this many books around me it almost feels like Christmas.

A shiver runs down my spine. In the summer I agreed to come home, back to Cornwall's west coast, for Christmas. Just for the week. But I have no idea how I'm going to be ready for it. The new school building we're working on is behind schedule, and without me being here to oversee it, a week's absence could delay the opening day even further. I'd at least like to see the roof on before term finishes.

I still have to buy my flight, too. I could just imagine Mum's face if I didn't turn up. I've spent Christmas either in South America or Asia for the last few years. It's difficult being the only one not in a relationship. And my family has grown dramatically in the last couple of years. I much prefer solitude.

Before I can spend any more time thinking about rooftops or Christmas festivities the early arrival children wander into the classroom, their parents on the early shifts at work. The rubbing of the eyes subsides once they realise what I'm opening, though, and they crowd around my desk and the books seeing which ones they're going to read first. I ask a couple of them to add the books to the bookshelves, and return to my teaching tasks of checking chalk supplies and mini blackboards. We'll hopefully have enough until the end of term.

I still have ten days before I have to make a decision on staying away for another

Christmas, or travelling halfway around the world with money that is needed here.

At the end of the school day, after the last child has left the room, I tidy up the class ready for tomorrow, the final day of the school week. I'm due on the new school site, also in southern Quito, in about an hour, so I have enough time to head to my apartment for my own lunch. I like the quiet of my own space. I spend so much time around other people that being by myself feels like a rare treat. At least twice a week I have lunch at home, with no meetings or work.

 I can't settle for my usual twenty minute nap, though. There are too many thoughts running around my head about how I can get out of going home for Christmas. Or at least reduce the time I'm away. I wish I wasn't always such a people pleaser; I forget to please myself sometimes.

Nancy

'Joe, come and give me a hand with these parcels.'

My husband, of almost 35 years, is right next to me, lifting the first of four parcels that have just arrived by courier– one new bike for each of the grandchildren. Well, little Emily has a balance bike, which I'm sure her Daddy will have her on before breakfast on Christmas morning, wheeling her around the garden. Charlotte's bike is decorated with unicorns, and ribbons, with a little basket on the front for her teddy. Ben and Olivia both have new mountain bikes so they can explore beyond the Lizard and Kynance cove with their Dad and Uncle – who also have new bikes waiting for them. I couldn't resist. I used to love everyone going for a walk and a cycle on Boxing Day. I'll potter along the coastal path with Joe and the girls, while the adventurers whoop and squeal all along the cliff tops, along with other families in the area. I love the guest house when it's full of tourists, but that's nothing compared to a house full of family.

Joe has manoeuvred the last of the parcels into the garage and joins me in the kitchen. The kettle has just boiled.

'Is it time?' He asks, reaching for the biscuit tin.

'Almost.' I turn the radio on and the familiar quiz music has just started. I select a digestive to dunk into my tea, and Joe heads straight for the chocolate bourbons; no dunking. For the next fifteen minutes we answer questions about fifty years of music, and calculate our scores. Joe beats me in both rounds today, but I don't mind; his sons get their competitiveness from their dad, and their compassion for others from me. I love spending time with the man I love, even after all these years together. Of course, by dinner time he'll have driven me crazy at least once.

I clear away the tin and put the cups in the dishwasher ready to switch on after lunch. I reach for the giant Christmas pudding notepad from the fridge, and the fluffy Santa pen that Olivia bought me last Christmas.

Okay, time to see where we're at with the list.

I'm just waiting on the final under-the-tree gifts – brand new books – which should be here by the weekend. The beds have all been made up, and towels all lay out on the beds. Cain and Lucy are due to arrive first, on the 18th, which is only in ten days. They'll have a couple of days to get over the jetlag before Jason and Shelly turn up, with middle-teen Ben and new-teen Olivia. Then Cassie should be flying in shortly after. I'll have to chase her for flight details so we know what time to pick her up. Cain and Jason can head over to Heathrow together. It's been too long since they had a proper catch up, what with living so far apart. I just hope they don't pick on Cassie all the way back home – although she can take care of herself against her brothers. I'd like to think they'll have outgrown pranking each other, but I know my children too well. Ben and Olivia only had a brief insight into their Dad and Uncle's relationship in the summer, in between Cain's shows, and off-duty Cain loves nothing more than winding his siblings up.

I clutch my chest, a grin dancing across my face. I can't wait to have the whole family together, even if it's just for a short time, before they all go their separate ways again. I suspect Cassie will be gone by New Year.

I tick the done items off the checklist, and head to the cellar to check on the drinks.

There's more than enough white and red, for meals and evenings. Could do with more Bailey's, though, as Cassie enjoys her Christmas drink. Cider and beer stocks are okay. Will add another couple of crates of champagne to the list. Joe can head over to the wine merchants tomorrow to pick the items up. I open the supermarket app on my phone and add orange juice to the list. Then it's time to make lunch.

The persistent ringing of a phone pulls me from an afternoon doze in my armchair. I look over at Joe who is also fast asleep. A quiz programme plays silently on the television. I reach over for the handset.

'Hello?'

'Nancy, it's Lucy.'

'Oh, Lucy, is everything okay? Is everyone okay?' Lucy always arranges our chats for after the girls have gone to bed. I sit up, and my sudden movement jolts Joe awake.

'We're all okay. I'd hoped to catch you today, instead of waiting.'

My sixty years on this planet, especially the last thirty as a parent, have taught me to hear in someone's voice when something is on their mind. I love Lucy like a daughter. She's the sweetest soul, and makes my Cain so very happy. And they've given me two wonderful grandchildren. Patience is an understated virtue.

I listen to her talk about her family, pride clear in her voice, with just the tinge of tiredness that comes from having a new baby.

Em. I should have guessed.

I fill her in on how my latest craft project is doing. Then she says it.

'Nancy, I'm really sorry to do this, but would you mind awfully if you came to us for Christmas instead?'

Images of Christmas Cornish high teas and blustery coastal walks, rounded off with evenings of board games and Baileys cream liqueur pass fleetingly through my mind.

'Of course not, dear. Is everything okay?'

The truth tumbles out then.

'Oh, Nancy, you are wonderful. That would mean the world to us. To me. Em hasn't been sleeping at all well these last few months, and the thought of all that travel with a grumpy baby. Even shared, the looks from everyone on the plane would be mortifying. I really thought we'd be okay.'

'It's okay, Lucy. I understand.' I close my eyes briefly, release a slow breath, and settle into my armchair. Joe stretches awake and heads to the kitchen; he's a good man. 'Now, what's the plan?'

If there's one thing that Lucy is, it's a planner.

Cain will book our flights, and he'll get hold of Jason and Cassie to explain the change of travel plans, and sort out their tickets, too. His Manager, Sarah, had sorted out all the UK flights, and they're refundable, so a spring visit from them to Cornwall could be on the cards. April offers better cycling weather, anyway.

When Lucy asks about any preparations that have already been done I downplay it. I was a Mum to two, once, before the livewire that is Cain came along. And Joe was home more than Cain is. I know Christmas is hard on Lucy, too, and her sister Elle. She'll be in Thailand with Jam this Christmas, so there will be room at the Nashville Narrators lodge for all of us. A Christmas experience in a log cabin will be a new adventure, anyway.

I reassure Lucy that everything is fine, ask her to pass on our thanks to Sarah for sorting out the flights, and ring off. Just as I'm wondering which charity will likely get the meat order I've paid for, and how quickly I can arrange for new bikes to be delivered to Nashville, Joe walks in with a tray of tea and cake. The Santa pen and pudding pad are lurking. He knows me so well.

'We're going to Nashville for Christmas then, love?'

'Aye, love. At least you won't have to play Tetris in the fridge for the meat.'

'And I won't be washing dishes until Boxing Day.'

We finish our tea and I make new plans for packing and travelling to Heathrow.

Week Two

15th – 21st December

Cassie

A howl wakes me and I snap upright in my bed, shoving the sheets to the side.

I fumble in bed for my phone, blinking as 0300 flashes on the screen.

Loud noises of nature are ring tones for my family, so I can act quickly if needed. I answer the call.

'Hmm?'

'Oh, Cassie, I've done it again, haven't I?'

'Hi Mum. Everything okay?'

'I always think you're further behind in time zones than you are. I thought you were going to bed.'

'It's okay. I needed to be up soon. What's up?' I crash back down on the bed and half-heartedly pull a sheet over me.

'Well, there's been a change of plans at Christmas. '

I listen to Mum talk about flights and Nashville and bikes and Boxing Day and thankfully she's brief, because I am so confused. Apparently, someone called Sarah will be contacting me soon about flights, and to let her know my UK flights. Which I still haven't bought.

After the call finishes I turn over. I could really do with another hour of sleep.

I don't know why I've been so stuck on this decision to buy a flight. After so many Christmas holidays spent away from home, I should be excited about seeing my family again, shouldn't I?

I swap sleeping sides in bed, so that I'm sleeping on my left. I bunch the duvet up and throw my right leg out of bed, my cotton floral pyjamas providing ample middle-of-the-night warmth; the duvet offers a comforting hug every now and then. It's been a while since I shared a bed with anyone, and I certainly don't need someone every night. Perhaps it's the idea of meeting up with so many couples over Christmas that stalled me on the ticket. All eyes will be on me, when is it my turn to settle down? Uh-huh.

It will be cool to see Jam again, the last surviving solo flyer - until he realised he's far too amazing to be single. And as long as Elle makes him happy that's all that matters. Lucy is cool, so her sister is bound to be.

I close my eyes and count backwards from 50, to find sleep. By the time I've done that eight times I give in and leave the comfort of my bed.

There is a ton of work still to do and if I'm now going to the US for Christmas, I have no real excuse to not turn up. And I can't turn up without gifts.

I take my phone into the kitchen, prepare coffee, and tap around in my calendar to include time for a quick shopping trip around the market. Coffee for the adults and chocolate for the kids will work, so I don't need to move my schedule around too much.

After I've drunk my first coffee and checked the day's schedule I head to the bathroom to shower and dress. Lessons this morning, checking on the new school building after lunch and shopping before dinner, so that I can assess how much space I need in my suitcase.

I dress in a simple and professional shift dress, leaving my damp hair wrapped up in a towel on my head while I make my last coffee of the morning and a breakfast of pancakes, adding chocolate to the bananas.

I switch on my laptop to check for emails which might make more sense than my early morning wake-up call with Mum. I probably should call her more often, if only so she'll at least she'll get used to the time zones.

To be fair to her, I have travelled to quite a few countries in the last decade, bouncing between Asia and Central America, teaching and raising funds for new schools. Education is not just taken for granted in the supposedly developed world, but for some people it's a place they actively discourage children to go to, knowing that work brings in immediate money. Bullies of all ages exist in schools, whether in staff or pupil format. Secondary schools are worse than primary schools, but at the younger age children's literacy still can slip through the net.

I believe in education for everyone, so that they can make the most of the amazing opportunities that this world has to offer. Maybe that's why I can't settle in the UK – I've seen too much. I'm needed in too many places.

My email notifications come through including one from a new contact.

Ah, the Sarah that Mum was talking about is Cain's manager. Makes a little more sense now about Nashville.

Sarah has asked if a flight going out to Tennessee on 22nd is okay, with a return flight for 2nd January. Possibly a slightly longer trip than I'd anticipated, but considerably less travel time. I can always check myself into a hotel for New Year, if being around everyone is too much, and work remotely.

I reply that she can go ahead and book my flights for 22nd and not to worry about cancelling any pre-booked flights.

I complete forty minutes of meditation and then walk to school.

Elle

I unlock my apartment door, which is a tricky affair, as Jam's arms are wrapped around my upper body. I love that he's taller than my five nine frame and how he towers over me.

We've just enjoyed an evening swim and are trying to get ready for another dinner with Don and Malee.

Soon; I love that he can't keep his hands off me.

I finally open the door and turn to face Jam, my arms resting on his shoulders. My phone vibrates on the desk and I glance over to see Lucy is video calling. Jam has also spotted it's my sister and he backs off. I toy with ringing her back later, but I'd never concentrate if I didn't make sure everything was okay.

Then I'll tell her about her timing.

'Yo, Sis.'

'Oh, Elle. I've done something daft.'

'What's up?' I pull out the chair and sit down.

'I've changed Christmas plans to Nashville. I couldn't cope with Em screaming on the flight.'

'Woah, woah, slow it down. Em okay?'

'Yes, just, well, teething. And not enjoying it. And letting everyone know.'

'Ah.' I am so not ready to parent. Jam waves at Lucy on screen, as he heads to the bathroom.

'So ... you're not going to Cornwall, then?'

'Nope, seemingly, I thought hosting Christmas here would be easier.'

'Ah, Sis, just consult your plan. You've got this. Thanksgiving went well, didn't it?'

'Yes, I am in full-on planning. And Thanksgiving was great. But, no presents, or decorations or tree or ....'

'Breathe, Luce. Where's Cain?'

'He's sorting out travel plans with Nancy and Jason. The phones have been going non-stop. I hope everyone can make it over.'

I chuckled. 'I can imagine the chaos.'

After ten more minutes of soothing my sister – I hadn't realised how bad her anxiety could get – I ring off.

I wish I'd spent more time with her when we were growing up, but there was never a right time. I was always over at friend's houses for Christmas, or working to save for studies.

We've seen each other more this past year than we have done in the last decade, and that's only been for a couple of months.

Jam appears in the bathroom doorway, a towel wrapped around his waist, in case Lucy is still on the screen.

'Oh no, you don't.' I said, unfolding myself from the chair, and pushing him backwards towards the shower. The towel drops and his hands help me peel off my bikini.

For the next couple of days I can only think about Christmas.

My dreams are filled with huge, wildly decorated Christmas trees, my beautiful sister and her family laughing and joking with their friends, whilst I look in through the window, unseen.

I bolt upright in bed, startled, as if I'd fallen from a fir, my breathing ragged. Lucy and her family growing away from me in another dream.

Jam lies snoring next to me.

We're still in Thailand. I slow my breathing down.

It will be Christmas in a week, one of the toughest times of his life, when he remembers his parents, who had sacrificed their lives. Of course I'd be with him, this year and every year.

I try to settle to sleep, but in actuality I just lie awake, listening to the sonorous sound of Jam, while I watch the sun rise through our window. And think of how far away I am from my sister. I've never needed Christmas surrounded by family so much. And this year they're celebrating in Nashville, and everyone is making the trip out.

How can I tell Jam that all I want for Christmas is to be in Tennessee instead of Thailand?

Eventually Sleeping Beauty stirs awake, immediately reaching out for me. I curl myself into his arms.

'Everything okay, Elle?'

I make a non-committal sound, not quite agreeing, not quite saying anything.

He strokes my hair and my arms and whispers how much he loves me, turning my sour start to the morning into a blissful one, at least twice. Just as the day is starting, I'm now ready for sleep.

Jam has the first shower while I'm curled up on the bed, wondering about the Christmas-themed painting project I'd started with the children on the island. Perhaps that's what had stirred up nostalgia, for Christmases I'd never really known.

Maybe next year we could celebrate with Lucy and Cain, instead of being in Thailand?

But that afternoon, once my classes had finished, I find myself in the apartment scrolling through a website for flights to Nashville, checking airport codes and locations against Google's directions. If nothing else I'm developing my geographical knowledge.

A message pops up informing me there is one seat left on a flight to Dallas, with a connecting flight in Tokyo. What am I thinking? What am I being told?

I watch Jam outside the window, chatting easily with Malee and Don. They've known him longer than I have; Malee has shared his pain, losing her sister in the Tsunami. I drag my eyes back to the screen and recheck the dates. I could be in Nashville just before Christmas Eve and be back on Boxing Day. It's insane and it's expensive. But it's something I have to do. I complete the payment before I lose the seat and let out a long breath. Maybe Jam will hardly know I've gone?

Maybe I won't go, and will just suffer the financial loss?

I log off and join everyone outside. Jam hands me a beer, reaches out to hold my hand. Malee smiles at us. How can I feel horrible and wonderful at the same time?

I throw myself into classes and celebrations over the next couple of days. There are just two expat teachers out here, from California. Jasmine is from Sacramento and Della from LA. They both met on the flight to Bangkok, and are pretty easy going people. So, along with Malee and Don, Jam won't be on his own for Christmas, anyway.

Besides, I haven't found the right way to tell Jam what I'm thinking.

He'll think I'm nuts, and he'll just have to trust that I can't quite explain my feelings anyway; I'll have one day with Lucy and then I'll be back with him. Couples take breaks apart from each other, don't they?

The next afternoon I pack my backpack whilst he's still teaching a music class and place the letter I've written on his pillow, including clues to one of his gifts; under the bed are 72 heart-shaped pebbles on my latest canvas painting, spelling out the words I Love

You, resting on the sand of our favourite beach.
 One pebble for each hour I'll be away.

Lucy

Cain is always reminding me that 1985's Live Aid, the first benefit concert of its kind and held in London and Philadelphia at the height of summer, was put together in six weeks. I look around the pages of lists in my notebooks that I've created; I should be able to pull together Christmas for eleven people in ten days, right?

Thank goodness Lottie is still in kindergarten for another week, and that Tallie has offered to help out with childcare. She's possibly also glad of the chance to stop fretting about spending Christmas with AJs huge, old-money family.

Cain walks through to the kitchen, drops a kiss on my forehead then refills our mugs with coffee.

'Hit me with the Christmas duties, Luce.' He nods to the spiral bound book in front of me.

'I thought you were still working? Don't you have the interviews at the station, about Bonnie and Patty's new song?

'There's no way I'm missing out on all this logistical fun. Plus, Bonnie and Patty said they could handle without me. And they'll be over later to help out.'

'Oh, we have the sweetest friends. And I have the sexiest husband.'

'Yeah, yeah. Tasks first.' He grins, sipping from his mug and wrapping his arm around my shoulder.

I flip the book open to the first list.

By the end of the afternoon, a Christmas in Nashville is starting to look good.

Patrick has sourced two turkeys for us, and added additional meat onto the order for the holiday meals. Thank goodness we have half-empty freezers in the lodge kitchen during this time of year – we'll be open again for writing retreats in January, so there's plenty of time to restock.

Patrick has also volunteered to stay working for an extra few days to minimise our holiday cooking time, and I know that means additional desserts. Some chocolate peppermint fudge and his festive holiday cupcakes would be perfect pick-me-ups, for as long as the delicacies lasted. His wife, Laurel, our Head Housekeeper, has promised to help us decorate the lodge.

I hear Cain singing *Deck the Halls* along the corridor, and I smile, enjoying his impromptu a capella. He appears moments later carrying a couple of plastic lidded boxes of decorations, the broadest smile on his face, wearing the reindeer antlers on his head that we bought last year for Lottie. He places the boxes on the floor in the living room, and repeats the trip, his vocals as smooth as the local honeyed whiskey. Eventually all the decorations are up from the basement.

'Is it beginning to feel a lot like Christmas?' He asks, pulling me towards him for a quick slow dance. I nod, smiling, then peek at the red and white and gold and sparkly catastrophe before us. Cain nods and starts to hum the Bing Crosby classic.

'Oh, it's like Christmas ate too much. Yet I know it's not enough.'

I reluctantly pull away from him and we start unpacking the boxes, planning where we could hang and dangle the tinsel and lights. And I add buy more decorations to the list.

I know Nancy loves decorating the guest house, so I really want to make her feel right at home in our own, albeit hastily cobbled together, Christmas land. I don't have quite as many snow globes as she does, though. I love hearing her stories about each of the 30-something globes she has either collected or been gifted every year since her children were small. I love the musical globes most. That twinkle of music seems to add to the magic of the perfect snow scene.

I've been so worried about sorting travel and sleeping arrangements that I simply haven't thought about decorating the lodge properly, with garlands and oversized candy canes and cosy knitted blankets.

We'll go shopping for additional decorations and trees tomorrow.

Tallie walks through the back door with Lottie and Em a few minutes later, and they all go crazy over the decorations and share excited giggles about shopping for trees; Lottie wants hers to be covered in snow. Maybe one year we'll be in the Canadian mountains and she will have real snow for Christmas.

'That looks quite a set of Christmas planning sessions you have there, Lucy. I'm happy to help out if you'd like an extra pair of hands.'

'Aren't you and AJ planning your first Christmas together?'

Tallie's cheeks redden and I pop my pen down. Briefly.

'We're going to his parents. In Boston. I'm so nervous, I could use the distraction.'

'You have nothing to worry about – you are wonderful to be around, they're going to love you. What gift have you bought for his parents?'

'A few months ago I asked your sister to create a painting of their favourite Robert Frost poem – The Road Not Taken – as she studied at Harvard I thought she'd be able to offer a personalised insight. It arrived last week.'

'See, you are so thoughtful, you really have nothing to worry about.' I smiled. Then added, 'And yes, another pair of hands are definitely most welcome, thank you!'

Patrick came in a little time later and my nose immediately stood to attention.

'Sliders? And sweet potato fries. Barbecue sauce and relish?'

'I thought you could all use a little culinary diversion.' Patrick smiles. 'I can make a batch of these for arrivals day next week, as a little snack before a ham dinner?' I nod, my eyes bright at having found Patrick only a couple of years ago. The writing retreat just wouldn't be the same without the dinners and breakfast he serves. 'You and Laurel are a heaven to this place, thank you!'

The smell of burgers brings everyone into the kitchen.

'There are turkey sliders, too, for Miss Lottie, and more than enough for everyone.'

'Patrick, you are star chef of the week!' I hug him and reach over for a cheeseburger. 'These will be perfect for next week.'

After dinner and decorating, Tallie and Cain bath the girls while I update the lists. A few phone calls sorted out travel arrangements – Sarah and Bonnie will help Cain to ferry the family from the airport when they arrive in just a few days' time.

The biggest job left to do is buy presents for everyone.

I had planned on an Amazon spree in the UK so we wouldn't have to pack everything. Now we had visits from Santa to arrange, including leaving milk, mince pies – Santa was particularly keen on cranberry and sultana pastry delicacies - and chocolate chip cookies out and footprints and hoof prints to leave outside. I sent out a group chat request to see if anyone wanted to go gift shopping soon at the Opry Mills mall, and it seemed I wasn't the only one last minute shopping. A shared afternoon was found for a shopping trip.

I'd heard about shopping for Christmas trees, but never actually appreciated how wonderfully sensory the experience was. The pine scent and stunning displays were magnificent. It was so much fun, I imagine, like walking through Santa's village, as he personally approved the selection of the perfect tree, or two – we were having one at home, and one at the lodge. Lottie was in her element running among the little forest, exuding oohs and aahs at every tree.

We'd topped up our decorations from the craft stalls, buying wooden nutcracker soldiers and a choir of freestanding snowmen as well as more garlands, for the stairway of the lodge. A crafter had three huge, red, arm-knitted throws, made from the softest yarn, so I bought all of them for Nancy's, Shelly's and Cassie's rooms. Cain spotted a charcoal knitted blanket and added that to the order, too. It would look perfect on our bed.

Lottie stopped moving suddenly, absolutely silent for the first time all month.

We turned to see what had caught her eye.

A fir, branches lush and green, and so tall, stood before her, covered in snow. Lottie was silent just long enough before she let out an excitable squeal.

Apparently, we've found our tree.

Cain bought three trees, deciding to have one in our hallway, too, and extra cans of the snow spray to make sure the branches always looked perfect.

As we wait for collection, we're sat around a wooden picnic table near the play park, enjoying hot chocolate and marshmallows. Em contemplates her new surroundings from Cain's arms while Lottie runs around burning off her endless energy playing with the other children in the park, her blonde hair flying in the wind.

'This feels like the calm before the storm, doesn't it?' I say, sipping my dark chocolate drink, licking my moustache away.

'This will possibly be the quietest time we have together for the next couple of weeks.' Cain agrees, setting Em on her feet so that she can watch her big sister do things she only dreams about as yet. Her tiny little fingers grip her Daddy's so tightly, it's hard to believe she's standing at just ten months.

Cain glances up at me, catching my reverie, and just smiles, nodding.

'Our little family is growing up.' He wrestles free from Em's grip, briefly, to wrap an arm around her waist, which she gleefully hangs onto, giving her arms a rest. He reaches out for my hand, and I smile at the security of our fingers together.

It feels like the world stills around us, just from holding hands.   Lottie bounds over then, chatting away, slurping her chocolatey milk. I manage a quick cuddle from her before she bounds back into the play park.

'Five more minutes play.' Cain advises. Then he squeezes my hand and walks Em over to join her big sister.

I snap a few more photos of the three of them, building my catalogue of memories. Just a couple more, by the decorated trees this evening, and the first part of my present to Cain will almost be ready.

That evening, snuggled on the sofa next to Cain, watching the Muppet Christmas Carol for the second time that day, I ticked off the jobs on today's lists, and read through my notebook jobs for tomorrow. Cain is hosting Daddy Day Care, likely with help from Seb, while I hit the mall with the girls – I was originally just going with Sarah, but Bonnie, Patty and Tallie are now taking on the mall madness, too, and have offered to help me buy my gifts as well as their own.

Bonnie has promised not to mention cocktails until all the presents have been secured. But we all agreed in the motivating force of her cranberry margaritas and clementine martinis, and I added taking advantage of store gift wrapping services to our lists – there was no way we'd be in a position to wrap once Bonnie hit the blender.

I was buying gifts for Shelly, Jason, Nancy and Olivia. Patty was buying for Ben and Joe, Tallie was buying for Patrick and Laurel. Bonnie was buying a gift for Sarah and Seb, and Sarah was buying for Patty and Bonnie. We agreed on two hours' shopping time and arranged to meet for gingerbread lattes at a coffee shop. Last one back was buying the food delivery tonight; Patrick was taking a couple of days off to sort out his own Christmas plans.

As we entered the fluorescent mall, Christmas trees and decorations and music seemingly pouring out of every shop window and doorway, I momentarily considered reverting to a quick online shop. The colours and noise were in such sharp contrast to our gentle family shopping trip buying Christmas trees and handmade decorations. A huge igloo covered one end of the mall alley, a queue of children snaking around, screaming and waiting for their turn with Santa. Shoppers laden with too many branded paper bags pushed past our little group as we all took in the mayhem.

The reverie broke when our collective fight wins out over flight. We nod affirmative to each other; Bonnie mimics synchronising watches and we hurry our separate ways, heads down, shoulders forward.

I have no idea why my sister enjoyed shopping so much. I mean, she isn't as into malls as she had once been, but I'd heard her stories in defence of consumerism.

All I can say is that she clearly hasn't coordinated shopping in a mall, for double-figure gifts, in a two hour session.

People were spilling everywhere and shelves were bare in many stores.

And the Christmas songs didn't feel as festive against the backdrop of so much chatter and tinny announcements about mall security. I should have just stuck to my Amazon goals, but I didn't want to miss delivery by running an errand elsewhere. Sarah had convinced me if we each broke down the gift list, we'd have it done in a morning. She is clearly as out of the loop with malls as I am.

I've only bought a craft-inspired room ornament for Nancy and a fancy cosmetic kit for my sister-in-law. I have no idea what to buy a new teen – I figured that the toy section is out, and I don't really know what Olivia is into. I could message Shelly, but I don't want her to think I'm so disorganised.   I head to the chocolate section for Jason, who I know has a sweet tooth for Ghirardelli chocolates. But I still have nothing for Olivia, and my two hours are almost up.

I'm seriously considering a Yankee Candle gift for my teenage niece when Bonnie and Patty tear past me, grinning, wearing matching Santa hats, on their way to the gingerbread lattes. I think pizzas are on me tonight.

After three more stores my head throb turns feral and I give up, heading towards my gingerbread latte, for a refuel and a rethink. If

I only have one Amazon delivery to wait for it won't be so bad, will it?

The girls, all wearing Santa hats, sat at a couple of nearby tables, surrounded by bags and laughter. It was the right kind of balm to the horrors of the mall I'd just experienced.

Patty held out a hat for me as I sank into my seat, a latte already waiting, alongside a slice of peanut butter cheesecake.

'Oh, God, I forgot Cassie.' The horrors were back.

'Would she like a couple of novels? I bought these for my parents, but then found a glassware set I'd rather give them.' Tallie offered.

'That would be brilliant, thank you – she does enjoy reading.' I took the books, Venmo'd the money across to her and bit into the cheesecake.

'Does anyone need an eye palette? I bought one for myself, but realised the colours are a little young looking.' Patty said, waving around a high end make-up product, which a teen would probably love.

'I think I could just have sat here and let you all shop, you're so good.' I grinned. 'Dinner for everyone is definitely on me tonight, I couldn't have done this without you.'

'I love targeted-shopping.' Bonnie declared. 'So much more time for drinking'.

'I love this woman.' Patty yelled, throwing her arm around her shoulder.

When we return home, I store the gifts in my office, noting that only a couple will need to be wrapped, and then find Cain in the studio with Lottie banging on the drums. Her Uncle Jam would be so proud.

Em crawled around the studio and Cain held his finger to his lips, to indicate he was recording. I realised Lottie was playing the beat to Little Drummer Boy, and she kept a pretty steady time, her face furrowed in concentration. She finished with a flourish and Cain paused the recording, taking his headphones off. He held up double thumbs and Lottie scrambled off the kit and into the studio.

'Is it finished, Daddy? Can we show Mummy?'

'Why don't you take Mummy into the dining room while I finish up here?'

I gave Cain a quick kiss, scooped Em up and followed Lottie through to our dining room. Paper chains hung across the table, and hand cut snowflakes, from white paper, decorated the doors.

'Did you do these?' She nodded happily, showing me everything she'd done, and I gave her a big hug. 'You are a brilliant Christmas decorator.'

Nancy

'How much luggage allowance can we take again?' I yell at Joe from the bedroom. I can barely see the bed for the wrapped presents I'm trying to shove into submission in all of our Antler cases. The presents all seem to be just too big to fit more than one in.

Joe wanders through, reading from a print out, his glasses perched on the end of his nose.

'It says here, up to three bags, totalling 32kg, is included. Then we can pay for anything after that.'

'It's the carrying, not the money, I'm thinking about. Why does the packaging on children's toys have to be so bulky? I know for a fact that I can reduce the size of these things. Unwrapping it is.' I reach in for a large rectangle box - a set of unicorns for Charlotte; two tiers, lots of space in between. My three favourite snow globes, still in their original boxes, are lined up next to each other, barely taking up any room.

'Now, wait a minute.' Joe gently removes the box from me. 'Let me see what I can do.'

He glances at the globes and smiles at me, knowingly then continues examining the case.

'The first globes the children ever bought us.'

I stand back and watch as he examines each of the parcels, testing their structure and weight distribution in his hands. Like feeling the muscle memory from hearing a familiar song, I'm transported back to a Christmas that doesn't feel so long ago, even though I have Grandteens now.

Jason, Cassie and Cain presenting me with their gifts of little snow scenes that they'd seen at a Christmas market in Plymouth one year. We'd just been to the theatre to see a production of The Gingerbread Man. Jason had been too old, but Cain and Cassie had loved the performance; they'd all enjoyed the gingerbread treats I'd snuck in my bag to enjoy during intermission.

On the way to the railway station for the journey home we'd stopped at the wooden hut stalls on the piazza, selling handmade gifts and the most delicious food. I kept turning the keys on snow globes, gently shaking them and watching the snow slowly descend, supposedly to entertain the children, but I'd always loved the perfect worlds contained in the glass spheres. Suddenly Jason was dragging me away asking for a hot dog, and Cassie and Cain had promised to stay at the stall together.

That had been their first ruse I hadn't had to tell them off for. Three snow globes, presented by my mischievous angels. A snowman in one, a little train and Christmas tree in another and Father Christmas and his reindeers in the third. They hadn't been able to agree on one, so Cain had suggested buying one each, and had apparently got a good deal from the stall holder.
I sigh wistfully.

Engineer-Joe seems to know what he's doing, and I decide it's definitely time for tea and biscuits.

Joe joins me a little while later, and I pour his tea from the teapot. He takes out a chocolate Bourbon biscuit.

'Well, the children's presents are in. No unwrapping needed. I turned the large presents diagonally and worked around them. If we're creative on clothing, we may even get to wear more than one outfit each over Christmas, that isn't the pyjamas I know you've packed for everyone.'

'Oh, well done, Mr Adams. I would have hated to have unwrapped and unboxed everything. I'm also very glad there are only two little children; presents are definitely smaller the older you get.' I dunk a digestive biscuit in my tea and consult the next Christmas-pudding shaped list.

'Ah, I'm going to ring Shelly after this, to find out if they have room for any of Cain's favourite Cornish Rattler cider, and Lucy's favourite Cadbury's.

Three more sleeps

Elle

How had I not anticipated heart-wrenching, snotty, ugly tears at the airport, alone?

Or how hard it is to emit quiet, heartbroken sobs, without attracting unwanted attention?

Thank fuck I packed my sunglasses and my headphones. I feel like I'm a fault line, with one piece of my heart in Thailand, the other in Nashville. As my body shudders another round, I rub my sweatshirt sleeve under my glasses, the damp, cold cotton no more than I deserve. This is the longest time I've been away from Jam since early summer; I really ought to get a grip, right?

I look around for distraction. The airport is full of travellers, toting huge cases. I'm so glad I don't have to wait by the baggage claim when I get to Dallas. Straight into the hire car across the country to my birth family. I'm going to blast out the loudest country music heartache songs to keep me upright. At last the genre is starting to make sense.

I didn't think I had any tears left in me, but a fresh wave hits and I turn towards the window, looking over the tarmac. Our flight is boarding, the queue of passengers haphazard around cluttered chairs. I'm going to be the last passenger on, and the very first passenger off. The queue shuffles forward and I stare out of the window at Thailand. People are entering peak tourist season, dressed in flip-flops and shorts. It doesn't feel at all Christmassy. As the sky darkens the silhouette of the slowly-moving passenger queue behind me means that I don't have to turn around to know when it's clear enough for me to board.

I can't look at any of the other passengers face on.

I know they can see the tears streaming beneath my glasses, hear the sobs, see my shoulders wavering.

What have I done?

I need to turn around, go back to Jam, tell him that I've been such a berk, but I missed Lucy so much.

But if I miss this flight I won't be able to spend Christmas with her.

Maybe I should just go out in January for a week?

I've never felt so numbed with pain.

I stare through the window at the changing day light.

Passengers are still boarding. There's still time.

To do what?

A familiar outline appears to be walking towards me and I grip my eyes shut against the onslaught of dry tears. Then I fling them open in a reality check when his scent hits me.

I'm not hallucinating.

I spin around.

Jam catches me before I fall, my flailing limbs knocking into him. My hands grip the collar of his shirt.

I don't know whether he's angry or sad and I really just want him to be angry.

'Elle.'

'Jam.'

'Do you know how many speed limits and laws I broke getting here?'

I shake my head, still gripping onto him. He pulls us to the seat so I'm less precariously balanced. His arms tighten around me. His forehead presses into mine.

'I'm so sorry, Jam.'

'*You're* sorry? I'm sorry.'

'What are you apologising for?'

A hiccup interrupts my thoughts, and he pulls me closer, his fingers running through the strands of my hair. How can I be in my happy place and hell at the same time?

'I should have noticed you weren't okay. I wish you'd told me what you were feeling. Do you know how I felt, seeing that note?' He whispers.

I look up at his grey face, my hand flying to my mouth. Shit, it looked like a break up letter.

He holds me tighter, holds me together; his warm breath tickles my face.

'We're going back to Nashville together, Elle'.

'That was the thing... I could only buy one ticket, Jam.' Yet more tears spring forward. Jam rocks me slowly in arms I never want to leave again.

How could I have hurt this man, at this time of year?

I don't deserve him.

I can't live without him.

'There is no way we'll be apart for our first Christmas together. I called in every favour I've ever been promised, but we'll both be in Nashville for Christmas. And New Year. And for however long you want to stay there.'

'But Thailand. Boxing Day? Your parents?'

'We can spend Christmas - and Boxing Day - anywhere, sweetheart, as long as I can spend them with you. If you still want to?'

That last question upsets my tears even more than I thought possible. I nod furiously wrapping my arms around him even tighter.

A final call is announced for the flight and the attendant coughs nearby. I look around, blinking; we're the only passengers left.

Jam takes my right hand in his, his warm fingers around mine providing calm and support. He takes my passport in his right, handing it over with his to the woman with the broad smile. She nods and shepherds us through, before finally closing the gate.

At the entrance he pulls me left, towards First... so this is how he'd got a ticket. I perch on the end of his bed, intent on kissing him goodnight and heading to Economy.

'I think it's time for me to get to my seat.' This will be the longest flight.

'Yes, Elle, right here. Next to me. Always.'

He waves another ticket at me, and pats the bed next to him.

My heart. I sink down, legs trembling again. Then look up at Jam, losing myself in the heat of his dark chocolate eyes.

Well, someone's getting lucky tonight, whoever discovers they have an available Economy seat next to them on the overnight flight; Jam couldn't get any luckier.

Nor could I; love is holding on tight to the person you love, even when they lose themselves.

Nancy

'Put the phone down, Nancy. Jason will be driving, Shelly will be reading, and the kids will be watching their tablets.'

'Oh, I know you're right, but I just want to keep track of where everyone is. Do you think we'll get all of this luggage through? It took so long to pack, I'd hate to have to abandon things. I won't abandon things.'

Joe placed his hand reassuringly on my leg.

'Nance, trust your son.'

I sighed and put the phone in the empty cup holder.

'I know, I know, Cain has upped the luggage allowance for us, so we'll be able to take it all'. We had packed everything so well, and then I realised that I hadn't included the Christmas outfits and Cornwall edition of Monopoly that we always played on Boxing Day. All this had come out on the phone to Cain, double-checking if we needed to bring anything else - and he'd told us to bring everything and he'd increase the baggage allowance. I don't know why he insisted we arrive almost a day before the flight, though.

A message beeps through and I adjust my glasses to check my phone.

'Oh, it's from Olivia. *What are the best Christmas films* she's asking? *I'm updating my Netflix account and need ideas*.' I put the phone on my lap.

'Elf.' Joe declares. I remember we had that on every Christmas for Ben and Olivia a few years ago.

'You can't beat the classics – Miracle on 34th Street. From the 1940s. Although the Richard Attenborough remake was good. Ours were a little too old to appreciate the sentiment, though.'

'I quite liked Die Hard as a Christmas film.'

'I'm not sure Olivia is after creating a list of action films.'

'The underdog saves Christmas for everyone. And it snows. What's not to love?'

'Now, wait, why does it snow? Isn't it set in LA?'

'Ah, maybe I'm thinking of the second Die Hard film. But it has Christmas music in. And it's set on Christmas Eve.'

I reply to Olivia with our film choices, and stare out of the window as Heathrow approaches. The shock of the high rise concrete buildings is a stark contrast to our views of the Atlantic Ocean at the back of the guest house.

When we're on one of our cruises we sail from Southampton, which is huge in comparison to our little village in Cornwall. We've flown out to Nashville once or twice before, in the summer. Never at Christmas, when there is ice and snow to contend with, as well as gifts and traditions.

Admittedly there is no sign of snow. Just rain. I hope the cases won't get soaked being transported onto the plane. I don't think I used enough plastic bags to protect the presents. I have no idea what clothes I've packed – I was tucking everything in between gifts for our baby girls, and our big children – they will all know that Santa loves them very, very much.

Joe made the turn for our terminal parking. There was supposed to be a bus to escort us to departures, but we would wait for Jason and Shelly – I didn't want everyone to get lost inside the monster of a building.

We only had to wait a few minutes before Jason turned up. Ben and Olivia hugged us and reached for cases. Ben almost dropped our large one in surprise.

'What's in here, Gran, the Christmas turkey? Frozen?'

'Ben!' Shelly admonished.

'Oh, that's okay. Santa made an early visit to Cornwall, Ben.' Joe tapped the side of his nose and Ben grinned. He replaced his huge headphones and fished out the handle on our case, carting it along with his case. A weighted backpack wrapped around his back. He was taking after his Dad and his Uncle in the strength department – that's what comes from surfing and skiing holidays.

The rain had eased off, and we didn't have long to wait for the connecting transport, which was thankfully empty, so there was no struggle finding room for everyone and everything.

When we arrived at the departures area, Shelly took the printed tickets we handed her.

'Nancy, Joe, have you read these tickets?' She asked.

'Oh, what have we missed? We're on the right day, aren't we?'

'Yes, yes. We're in the right place. Almost. Jase, have a look at these will you?'

Jason inspected the tickets, Joe held on to my hand in that godforsaken fake-tree-lined airport.

'What, what?'

'This way, Mum, Dad. Kids.' Jason and Shelly led us to an empty desk.

'Oh, cool, we're going First?'

'We so are.' Olivia confirmed, tapping away on her phone.

'Is this your first trip to Nashville?' The attendant inquired, after we'd waved our luggage off.

'Our Uncle lives there. He's a famous singer. He bought us the First class tickets.' Olivia beamed.

'Oh, well, have a lovely time visiting family for the holidays. Just follow the signs there to the lounge. Enjoy your flight.'

What on earth was happening? I just wanted tea.

Another pristinely attired attendant held a door open for us and we entered a huge, beautifully decorated and serene room. A few people tapped away on keyboards, a glass of something in front of them. A much nicer affair than their main entrance.

Olivia and Shelly hugged each other and wandered off to explore. Jason and Joe found a seating area large enough for us all and sank down. I had a little read of the facilities available, quite glad Cain insisted on arriving here earlier than planned.

Olivia and her Mum were back to whisk me away. 'Come on, we're going to a little spa treatment. They've had a cancellation so there's room for us.' Shelly said. Jason shook his head, knowing they were never travelling anything other than First ever again.

Cassie

My bags were finally packed, and I knew where I was going. LA then Nashville for almost a fortnight, the longest winter break I'd ever taken.

I'd held Christmas celebrations with my classes, and assured the building contractors that I'd be back just after the New Year, and the school would open in February.

I'd emptied my fridge and bought and wrapped small gifts of coffee and chocolate from Ecuador. I was on my way to the bus for the airport when my apartment phone rang. Instinctively I picked it up.

'Cassandra, we need you,'

'Hello Mr Raul.' I sighed. The Head Teacher was always a little urgent-sounding. 'I told you, I'm going to see family for the holidays.'

'Oh, I know, but there is so much work to do. Can you spare just a few minutes to help out your colleagues?'

What impact would just a few minutes have? I know that those minutes would turn to an hour, at least. And then dinner. Which would be very kind, but I would definitely miss my flight. This call was already delaying it. When was the last time I had said no to helping anyone out? In Ecuador, in China, in Chile, in Japan. I always said yes. And it was tiring.

'I'm sorry Mr Raul, I really can't help now. I haven't seen my family at Christmas for so long. I really must see them. I wish you and your family well. Merry Christmas.' I replaced the handset and hurried out of the apartment before I had a change to rethink my actions. Airport, airport, airport. That was my focus.

And to see what First Class travel felt like; I was tempted to eat my weight in free food, just because I could.

By the time my final, much-delayed plane touched down in Nashville, I couldn't decide if I needed sleep, or another strong drink more. Even First feels rough when you cross time zones later than planned.

My eyes felt sunk into the back of my head and I prayed that Cain wouldn't want to talk too much on the journey to the kitchen/bed in which I needed to spend the next 12 hours.

He'd already text me the plate number of the car to look out for and I found it easy enough, but an incredibly gorgeous woman leapt out of the driver's seat, perfect blonde waves cascading down over her white leather jacket. She shoved her sunglasses on top of her head and came to retrieve my case.

'Hey, Cassie, right? I'm Bonnie. Cain gave me a message to tell you – are you ready?'

I nod, taking in the juxtaposition of our appearances.

'Hey Cass, I really wanted to pick up my big sis from the airport – and sing annoying Christmas songs to you all the way back home – but your other brother managed to catch the only other delayed flight, so times got mixed. Lucy's list has finally been abandoned – I saw Sarah tear it up for her own good. Anyhoo – he actually says that, not me – *this is Bonnie and she is awesome* – I am, but it's kind of him to say so - *and she will look after you* – I totally will. *Can't wait to see you.'* I'm also down for any Christmas singing on the journey. Just hit me up with your favourites.'

'Um, hi.' I finally managed.
Up close, Bonnie's skin was ethereal, practically luminous. As soon as I clear this jetlag, I'm drop-kicking my baby brother at the earliest opportunity. I could have freshened up on the plane had I known I'd be meeting a siren.

I climb into the passenger seat and Bonnie hops in, hitting the stereo system. She stops at a country station blaring out Christmas tunes. Automatically my hand flies to the off button.

'I'm really not a country music fan.'

'What? OhmyGod you are too funny.'

Bonnie exits the airport and dials the happy down a notch, switching to a station playing Christmas tunes, which she hums along too.

'It's been a while since I flew, and I think I've forgotten how noisy flights can be.'

'Yeah? Cain has talked about you so much I feel like I almost know you. How's Quito?'

'Hmm, good, thanks.' What the hell was wrong with me and sentences today?

'Furthest I've been is LA for an awesome show by Queen and Adam Lambert – but I drove so guess it's a little different.'

'Are you a musician?' I tentatively asked.

'Some. I also make a great cocktail.'

'Ah, I love pretty cocktails. Ugly ones will do at the right time.'

Bonnie has a musical laugh. I bet she'd make country music sound bearable. Well, Cain did, too, but he was my brother and it would never stop being weird hearing him sing.

We talked about favourite drinks and Christmas drink recipes all the way home. By the time I got in I was rewarded with my second wind.

'Siiiiiiiiiiiiis.' Cain flies into me, but I right myself. It feels good to see him again.

'You've aged, Cain. Oh, I meant well, you've aged well.' I duck his rib dive and fold his hands behind his back, tweaking his ear instead, like I used to do when we were little. I turn him in a circle until he calls for mercy, which he manages to do through shared hysterics with Bonnie.

I leave my case for him to deal with and wander through their front door in search of more family.

I find everyone by the fire in the living room in various stages of comfort, surrounded by blankets and cushions and hot chocolate. We're all feeling the lag, then. After more hugs than I'd had since summer, when I'd last seen everyone briefly, Bonnie came into the lounge bearing a tray of orange cocktails.

'Clementine Martini, everyone? The holidays in a glass.'

By the time I crashed out in my room at the lodge, I had no idea if it was the lag or the mixing that had me floored. Bonnie was so creative with her drinks, that, rather like a selection box of chocolates, you just have to go for one of each. Lucy brought out enchiladas and burritos at some point, and I think I remember eating some. But I had had So. Many. Conversations.

And not enough nearly enough with Bonnie.

Lucy

I sat quietly at the kitchen table with coffee and today's checklist page. We had three flights due to arrive, with nine passengers, before lunch, including a spontaneous visit from Elle and Jam, which I was so ridiculously happy about. All the gang would be together.

Cain, Sarah and Bonnie were on airport duties. Seb was on kitchen assistance, ensuring we were all fed and watered.

The guest house beds were made up to fend off the jetlag whenever people wanted. The trees and rooms looked over-the-top festive, like something out of a 24-hour Christmas movie channel. Charlotte and Emily had written their lists for Santa, and after a quick check I had sourced all their requested gifts, so I wouldn't need an emergency dash to the mall – the last visit had nearly floored me.

Or maybe that was just Bonnie's Christmas cocktails afterwards? I ought to stay away from that woman's mixology skills.

In just a few hours the house would be packed with family and noise and food and I couldn't wait.

'Hello, Mummy.' Lottie crashed into my lap, and Cain appeared a few minutes later with Em in his arms.

'Excited, much?' Cain whispered, leaning down to kiss me. I took Em from him, sitting her on my knee, whilst he organised breakfast for the girls, and I listened to Lottie ask questions about how Santa would know where to deliver Granny's presents to, because they'd all be in England.

I watched Cain create a gingerbread latte for me and Christmas tree-shaped pancakes for Lottie, pour himself coffee, while I enjoyed the calm before the storm of the next 48 hours.

The guest rooms at the lodge were already made up, with fresh Christmas-inspired bedding, thanks to Laurel's wonderful organisation skills. However, after watching a Christmas movie the other night with Cain I'd seen how decorations could really be used well in a room to make the guest feel so very festive. I'd hung lights in Ben's room, in the twin room Olivia would share with Lottie and in Shelly and Jason's suite. I knew Christmas was always a difficult time for Jam, and this was actually the first holiday we'd spent together, as he was usually in Thailand. A few lights would be okay, especially the cheesier decorations that were free of sentiment, just good fun. Like surfing Santas and tinselled flamingos, hopefully reminding my sister and Jam of all their travels. They could also stay at Jam's place, just a few minutes' walk away, if the chaos was overwhelming.

When it came to Nancy and Joe's room, though, I remembered how much gusto she'd given decorations in their guesthouse in West Cornwall. I'd placed a small fir tree in their room, named stockings hung on the wall, which I'd pop their gifts in on Christmas Eve, and garlands, lights, nutcracker soldiers, felted gnomes and mischievous elves were displayed everywhere. I'd hoped it was a crafters' Christmas, as every item had been handmade, not by me, but sourced from Christmas markets. Lottie had made some paper snowflakes which we'd put on the windows later.

After breakfast, I took the girls up to dress while Cain caught up with messages in his office.

Just before lunch time Sarah followed Cain to the airport to collect his parents, his brother and his family. Bonnie was due to collect Elle and Jam. Cain would return first, then set off to collect Cass when her flight landed in a few hours.

They all had lists, I had my central list; everything would be fine.

Except by three o'clock in the afternoon there was no sign of anyone.

Before Em woke from her nap, and while Lottie was watching a Scooby Doo Christmas special, I called everyone, eventually getting Bonnie on the phone.

'The flight from London was delayed, so Cain and Sarah set off about fifteen minutes ago. Elle and Jam got into a cab; think they just wanted to get to a bed as soon as – can't imagine the flight from Asia.'

'Oh, what a farce! As if airlines don't know the importance of Christmas.'

'I know, right?' Bonnie laughed. 'Cassie is due in half an hour, so I'll bring her back. And I have plenty of juice for the Christmas cocktails later on.'

'You're a star, Bonnie, thank you so much. You must have a ton of stuff to do this Christmas.'

'Ah, my folks have everything under control, and my sister is a bit of a control freak, so we give each other a wide berth sometimes. I like hanging out with you guys, if that's okay? Very chilled vibe.'

'Of course, it's great having you around! Thank you so much for picking Cass up. Oh, I think London has just pulled up. See you later, Bonnie. You get the extra pizza slice.'

'Win!'

I ring off to see Nancy and Joe get out of the car.

'Lucy!' Nancy calls out, holding out her hands for a hug. 'You look so well. Joe, doesn't she look well? Shelly, come say hi.'

I'd forgotten what a whirlwind Nancy is and it has been so long since we'd all been together as a family. I almost hoped that the jetlag would kick in soon so that people drifted to sleep in stages.

As we were bringing in luggage and catching up on flights – from their exuberant reminiscing, Shelly and Olivia loved flying First class - a taxi pulls up, and I hear Elle's squeals through the window.

I dive out of the melee to fling my arms around my sister.

It was so good to see her again, and for us to spend a Christmas together. The last time we'd been together, in Manchester, that's when she'd discovered I knew Cain. We were going to have the best Christmas holiday this year.

Christmas Eve Morning

Lucy

Christmas Eve is finally here.

I've woken early, before Lottie today, possibly more excited about Christmas than she is. I'm enjoying a quiet coffee at the kitchen table, watching the sun rise over our garden. The run up to today has been so different to what we all expected, but it's the next three days that matter. If it hasn't happened already then it doesn't need to. We're all here, we're all safe and healthy, there is plenty of food and everyone will have a gift to open tomorrow, if not several.

Later this morning Cain, Jason, Seb and Jam are taking the children off to the woods to look for reindeer clues; Seb and Jam will go on ahead creating fake snow prints and leaving ribbon and bells, for the children to find. Then Seb will circle back after Lottie and collect the woodland trinkets to leave out in Lottie's room, to help her plan to keep a sleepy eye open for Santa.

I look down at the last list I'll probably have to deal with this year – apart from the Christmas dinner timings tomorrow, although Patrick has done all the preparation. I just have to not burn it. Sarah and Seb will join us for dinner, so Seb could be persuaded to lend a culinary hand.

'Morning, Luce.' Cain reaches down to kiss me awake, his lips warm against mine, his hands cupping the back of my head. 'Couldn't sleep either?' He whispers.

'I think I'm probably too excited.' I smile. 'Are the girls still sleeping?'

He nods, pours coffee into his favourite Springsteen mug, the one from a show we saw in New York, just before Lottie was born. Cain had decided he was going to introduce me to gigs outside of country music. We'd made the most of our first year in the States together, while I adjusted to living with someone. I'd assimilated quickly after a long time on my own.

'Yeah, I figured they'd be pretty excitable for the next few days, so let them sleep while they can.'

'Last list.' I sing, waving my hand over the paper, which he takes from the table.

'Lottie and Em look for reindeers with the Dads, Ben and Olivia. Everyone else in the kitchen for baking.' He turned the paper over. Nothing.

'That's it?'

I nod and sip my cooling coffee.

'Geldof would be proud of the event organisation.'

'Takes a family to create something Christmassy, though. '

'It does indeed.'

'Morning Nancy.'

'Morning, Mum.'

Cain rose and filled the kettle with water to prepare the pot of tea which Nancy liked to start her day with. She was already dressed and ready for the day.

I pulled my robe a little tighter around me.

'Did you sleep well?'

'Like a log, dear, thank you. I must say I love the decorations in the lodge; that tree is spectacular, it smells divine. And the rooms look wonderful. I love being surrounded by Christmas.'

'I remembered. And I wanted to make up for not going to Cornwall.'

Nancy rested her hand on my arm.

'Don't you worry about the change of plans. As long as everyone is together – and we have tea.' She smiled at Cain as he set a bone china cup and saucer down, with milk and sugar. 'Then that's what Christmas is.'

'Christmas is beaches.'

I turned to see Jam and Elle wander in, dressed for summer, if not the cooler Nashville weather.

'Christmas is big.' Elle laughed, locking her fingers with Jam.

They made a cute couple. I was so happy they'd both made it over for the holidays.

I left Cain and Jam sorting out breakfast for everyone, while I slipped away to check on the girls and dress.

I found Shelly in Em's nursery, playing with her and getting her dressed. Olivia was helping Lottie brush her teeth and wash her face in their bathroom. I hugged both of my daughters and wished them good morning.

'Aww, thank you both so much.' I said to Shelly and Olivia.

'Not at all – I heard Em stirring, and Lottie was already awake. Olivia came in to see what I was up to and I roped her in for a little babysitting.'

Lottie's huge blue eyes were staring up at Olivia. I suspect if Olivia had asked her to do anything she would do it.

'It's great having us all together, isn't it? Now, you go and take time for you...there's enough of us to sort everything out.'

'Thank you, Shelly.' I smiled.

Back in our bedroom I lifted out the festive Christmas dress I'd bought for today. A jersey candy cane themed dress that I hadn't been able to resist when it popped up on my social media feed. I'd left baskets of Christmas themed hats and head wear around the house, so people could dress up or down if they wished. I'd managed to find everyone a silly Christmas jumper or dress that I'd give them tonight before bed.

Christmas had officially begun.

Breakfast was my favourite kind of great company and endless food. Cain just kept plating up bacon and eggs and pancakes, alongside lots of toast, and food disappeared faster than they could replace it. I offered to help, but he shooed me along with a smile.

After dishes were cleared, I got the girls ready for their adventure with the Dads and, after snapping endless photos, I closed the door on them. The quiet was instant. I smiled and headed back to the kitchen.

'Okay, okay, let's put on some Christmas music.' I yelled, asking our smart speaker to turn up the playlist I'd prepared. Dolly

Parton's unmistakable voice rings out through the room and I assign our baking tasks.

'Right, Elle, you're on gingerbread characters. Shelly, could you bake the cranberry muffins?'

Affirmative nods.

'Nancy, with your amazing craft skills could you work on a gingerbread house? I have plenty of icing sugar and sweets and candy canes.'

'Oh, absolutely, I haven't created a gingerbread house in years.'

'Brilliant. I'll work on a Yule log and mince pies.'

'I'd like to say we'll have enough food to last all week, but Jam has a tendency to forget to stop eating.'

I turn Dolly up and the kitchen starts to smell more incredible than bacon, pancakes and syrup.

'Shelly, after a quick lunch for the girls, Cain will put on the Polar Express for them. They'll be shattered after their reindeer search. Will Olivia and Ben be okay with that?'

'Oh, I love that film! Olivia still watches it now. Ben is "Elf" all the way, but he'll probably enjoy the nostalgia.'

'I can't wait until Lottie enjoys watching The Muppet Christmas Carol – she dives under a cushion when Jacob and Marley appear. '

'Oh, wow, Lucy, that's our childhood Christmas right there! Both of us under your duvet watching singing frogs and pigs every day up until Christmas!' Elle laughs, kneading gingerbread into a rough ball shape.

'When mine were little we watched Santa Claus the Movie, and Miracle on 34th Street. Until they discovered Gremlins. There's something a little surreal about watching a small town disintegrate thanks to monsters, while you're decorating a tree and waiting for Santa.'   Nancy stirred the icing sugar mixture.

'I remember being terrified by Gremlins,' said Cassie. 'Cain and Jason overrode me a lot when we were younger. I do remember watching It's a Wonderful Life a lot with you, Mum.'

'Oh, that's such a wonderful film.'

'Absolutely, Nancy, definitely one of my favourite films to watch.' I agreed. 'Much better to curl up with that classic than the Die Hard Cain insists on watching. Even if it is an 80s film.'

'Nope, the ultimate Christmas film of the 80s has to be Trading Places.' Said Shelly, scooping the cranberry muffin batter into the bun cases. 'Which I guess is sort of like a take on It's a Wonderful Life. What would happen if you had a different life?'

'I'd travel more.' All eyes turned to Cassie.

'You mean, more than the different-country-every-year?' asked Elle, voicing our thoughts.

'Yes, I do visit a lot of countries, but I stay there all year. I'd love to just go for a wander, seeing a different beach or mountain every month. Like you and Jam do, Elle.'

'So why don't you?' Shelly asked. 'I've never regretted the trips we've managed to take'.

'I guess I also like having a base, somewhere to plan my travel from.'

'You have one of those in Cornwall, dear' said Nancy, hugging her daughter, keeping her sticky hands just above Cassie's shoulders.

'And here in Nashville, any time.' I offered, smoothing chocolate buttercream alongside the chocolate sponge roll.

'There's also Cheshire. Or, Manchester, if you prefer.' Shelly joins in, dancing along to Merry Christmas, Everyone, one of my favourite Christmas songs, from Wales' own Shakin' Stevens. An 80s classic, of course.

'Ah, now that's the spirit of Christmas' said Elle, joining in the dancing as she added more jelly tots to the gingerbread house. Possibly to replace the ones she'd enjoyed.

'I liked the Miracle on 34th remake in the mid-90s, starring Richard Attenborough.' I said. Then I couldn't help adding, 'Did you know that 80s film legend John Hughes wrote the screenplay? And he was responsible for Home Alone, which I might have to watch with Lottie over the holidays.'

'Do not let Lucy loose on any film trivia competition over the next few days – we'll all lose with hardly any effort' Elle laughed, popping one of the sweets intended for the gingerbread men into her mouth and poking her tongue out at me.

'Now, now, children' said Shelly, then immediately clamps her hand over her mouth, as we all dissolve into laughter.

I added another dusting of icing sugar to the chocolate Yule log that was looking okay. It would be the only snow that we'd have this year. Maybe one year we'd head to Scandinavia with the girls and see real snow in its natural habitat.

Once Em could be distracted by films on a flight, like her big sister.

Lottie definitely had my DNA when it came to being distracted by film. It would only be a few more years before I could introduce her to classic 80s children's films, like Back to the Future, Karate Kid, and possibly Gremlins!

Suddenly, energy burst through the front door, in the form of rosy-faced children and their grown-ups, wielding hats and scarves and gloves and boots, by the sound of it.

I put my palette knife down and headed into the hallway, hanging coats up.

Cain bent down to kiss me, his lips chilled like a Martini. He had a twinkle in his eye that sent goose bumps down my spine.

Through Lottie's excited chatter I gather they'd found eight separate reindeer tracks.

'And we found bells, actual sleigh bells. We're going to leave them in my bedroom tonight so that when Father Christmas delivers some presents he'll see his sleigh bells and pick them up and put them in his – Dad, do you think Father Christmas has pockets in his suit?'

'I'd say he would have, otherwise where's he going to put his cookies?'

Lottie nodded, satisfied and carried on her ninety-mile-an-hour story. Olivia asked if she'd like to wash up together and Lottie charged up the stairs; she rarely has that much enthusiasm for the bathroom!

'Did you all have a good morning?' Cain asked, following me into the kitchen, lurking a little close to the chocolate Yule log. I gave him the look I reserve for student excuses about why they can't submit work on time, and he reaches for the sweets that Elle has been eating.

'Just lovely.' Nancy answered. 'How was your morning?'

'We lost Jam at one point...clearly he was too far from a beach to have any sense of direction ... Seb found him standing contemplatively by a tree.'

'I was listening out for sleigh bells.' Jam answered, coming in to help Elle and Cain eat the brightly coloured sweets. We were going for the minimal look gingerbread family, apparently.

It was time for a tea break anyway.

Christmas Eve Night

Cassie

It might feel weird hearing my baby brother's voice on the radio, and even though he is singing country songs, I'm always impressed at how he can hold a room.

After dinner Bonnie had popped over with gifts for the girls and she hadn't needed much persuasion to start mixing her Christmas cocktails. Then a few more people had stopped by, to wish Lucy and Cain Christmas greetings. They'd found themselves sidetracked by free-flowing food and Bonnie's apparently legendary Christmas in a glass.

I have to hand it to Nashvillians, too, they certainly know how to play music. Patty, Bonnie's friend and a songwriter that Cain works with, is an incredible storyteller with a voice that sings effortlessly of murder and mayhem. She just knows how to play the emotions as well as her guitar.

Jam has lived up to his nickname and from the smallest percussion set has produced a range of beats for Christmas party songs and traditional carols. At one point my littlest niece, Lottie, joined in with his infectious playing.

Seb brought in the banjo, for a bluegrass set, and another couple of musicians turned up with a steel guitar and fiddle. Maybe country music is meant to be played live, with family and friends gathered around a room, instead of just a noise on the radio that detracts from the skill involved. There are hundreds of years of this music within the mountains of Tennessee, Kentucky and Virginia, long before radio came along.

Bonnie walked past me, lightly touching my elbow and smiling, as she placed her cranberry margarita on a table, and sat at the piano. I leant against the wall, cradling a Cornish cider I'd swiped from Cain.

Her long fingers started playing a Christmas tune that I recognised as Hark! The Herald Angels Sing, and then she began to sing.

Her voice was so clear, it was like her vocal chords were made for the purity of carols. People moved closer to her and she was completely oblivious to everything except the song. I hoped nobody would stand before me because I was transfixed by her voice as well as her presence.

She broke my concentration with a hefty blues rhythm on the keys, to round off the song, whooping and reaching for her glass, coming out of the trance of the moment and being startled by the attention. But she took it on, sipped her drunk and launched into O Holy Night. Cain moved closer to sing harmony, and Seb added a light guitar accompaniment. My cheeks were blushing furiously, whether from the talent or the cider I wasn't entirely sure. I did not want this night to end.

I sense Mum join me, coffee in a reindeer mug warming her hands, although I felt plenty warm.

Still the pathway to the piano was clear.

Mum nudged me with her upper arm and I found myself leaning between her and the wall as O Holy Night gave way to Elvis' Blue Christmas, Bonnie going full on Elton John on the keys.

'She's good, isn't she?' Mum asked.

'Hmmm? Oh, yeah, a very talented musician. She sings pretty well, too.' I raise the glass to my lips.

'She's a lovely person, too. Helped Lucy out lots with preparing for Christmas. Her own family live not far away. Mum. Brother. Sister.'

I turn to Mum, watching her eyes. She has that look in them that I've seen before. Like she knows something but isn't for telling until she's ready to.

I grew up with two brothers; I can play a long waiting game. Jason and Cain always caved before I did.

'Oh, it's so lovely to see you over Christmas. Thank you for making the trip. I half wondered if you'd be able to make it to Cornwall.'

I sigh and lean into Mum. 'I hadn't bought my flights for the UK. I guess I kept telling myself I had so much work on I couldn't take all that time off.'

'Maybe your Dad and I could visit you next year? Meet some of your friends.'

'That would be brilliant. The school will be up by then. I could get you a guest teaching spot. The kids would love hearing from you.'

'You're so animated when caring for others, Cass.'

'Hey, hey, hey.' Jam loped over, a beer in one hand and his other arm around Elle.

'That was just wonderful playing, Jam.'

'Thank you, Nancy.' Jam raised his beer to Nancy's cup and my glass, then to Elle's cocktail.

I heard the live music change; no more piano. I tried not to look for Bonnie as our group became larger. Shelly and Jason now joined us, reminiscing over previous Christmas Eve celebrations with younger children. Ben and Olivia were pretty cool, either playing with Lottie or chatting to someone. So many kids usually had their heads stuck in devices.

A familiar fruity scent caught my nose and I looked up to see Bonnie grinning over her glass at us.

'Did I hear a pub crawl mentioned?'

'Hey. Yes, I was just telling Shelly that we could go on a pub crawl one Christmas, now our children are older.'

'So, you crawl between pubs?'

'Well, maybe towards the end. You visit as many pubs as you can over the evening. Until heading home to finish any last minute toy DIY before Santa visits.'

'I may have to come to the UK one year if we're visiting pubs. Sounds perfectly quaint and lovely.'

'Ah, the cocktails won't be as delicious.' Shelly said, raising her glass.

'Thank you. What New Year traditions do you have?'

'Oh, more pubs.' Jason smiled.

'I think I would make a great Brit.' Bonnie laughed.

'What do you do?' Shelly asked.

'House parties. My sister is hosting this year – you should all come.'

Suddenly, thoughts of a quiet hotel room, working, didn't sound so appealing. I listened as my family shared their plans. But all I could think of: what would a whole evening with Bonnie feel like?

'How about you, Cass? Fancy cocktails and swishy clothes next week?'

I nod. 'Sounds good.' The two most non-committal words in the English language.

'Swishy clothes?' Shelly asks. 'I'm not sure I've dressed up in so long.'

'I have a ton of stuff you can borrow.'

'Sounds fun, Jam' said Elle, squealing as Jam wraps his arm tightly around her, pulling her to him.

'Sure. Sounds good.'

I looked at him from the side. He isn't holding eye contact with anyone.

Christmas Day Morning

Nancy

This is what Christmas is all about; family, laughing and remembering with each other.

I look over at Joe, sat in the opposite armchair and he smiles at me, that knowing smile of a lifetime together.

'Nana!' Lottie yells, waving the arm of a small doll towards me. 'Santa knew I needed another new dolly.' She cuddled the little girl close to her.

'Awww, Gran. I love the knitting kit. Now I'm a crafter just like you. Thank you. Can we make New Year's decorations? I loved making pompoms.'

'Of course, dear.' I breathe in Olivia's happiness, a miniature version of me, who really took charge organising the crafts and creating some unique yarn ornaments from the tree yesterday. She isn't all about technology, I'm glad to see. Unless she's eyeing up my sewing machine or die cutter, of course. Maybe next year I'll introduce her to the craft circle, really see how far her skills stretch.

'Oh.' Shelly paused in her unwrapping, her eyes shining at the photo journal on her lap.

'Ben and Olivia on every Christmas morning. Smile.' I snap a photo of my eldest granddaughter and her brother, almost grown up this year. 'Another one for the collection.' Lucy and Cain have yet to open their Christmas journal. Christmas is everything to me and I love recording the moments. Jason steps forward and hands me a book-shaped gift. 'Here you go, Mum,'

A glossy photo book falls into my lap. All of my grandchildren on all their Christmas Days.

I beam and stroke the images, with text underneath, to remind me of the years. 'Is that a high tech version of your journals?' Joe asks, shaking his head, with another knowing smile. He reaches for his glasses and I hand the book to him, smiling. I won't acknowledge his complicit actions just yet.

'Time for some Christmas music.' Cain states.

He presses a few buttons on his phone and the TV comes to life. The room offers a collective sigh as celluloid Lottie announces, 'Happy Christmas, Mummy.' The in-the-room Lottie dances around, as the video cuts to her sat at a small drum kit, starting the introduction to Little Drummer Boy. I glance over at Lucy and her eyes dart between the two Lotties, widening when they both begin to sing. On the T V the camera now includes Em, sat in the studio on her mat, shaking a tambourine in earnest. That breaks Lucy's spell and she joins her eldest daughter for a dance, swiftly followed by my youngest and his youngest, the four of them dancing whilst everyone is continuing to unwrap presents.

   We can't take our eyes off my youngest son and his forever love.

Lottie has finished opening her first round of presents, and has now decided that it's breakfast time. It's not even eight o'clock yet.

   Lucy, Cain, Elle and Jam are in the kitchen and the rest of us are seated in the dining room, according to Lottie's place settings that she decorated the other day, as part of our craft session. Olivia stamped the designs and wrote names in beautiful calligraphy, then handed to her cousin for the important colouring-in job.

   The smell of pancakes, bacon and coffee enters the room, and despite the earliness of the hour I'm hungrier than I realise. Ben plays Christmas music through his phone and a speaker in the room, in between forking huge chunks of pancake into his mouth, until we all agree on gentle Christmas carols for the hour.

I glance over at Cassie, a cup poised between her hands. She's watching her family, but perhaps thinking of something, or someone, else, as familiar songs played at last night's impromptu show, ring out around the room. I know it's a parent's wish to see all their children settle down with someone. For too many years Cassie has been on her own, transient friends that she leaves behind from one country to the next, and no long-term companionship to share her incredible adventures with. Maybe her time is closer than she thinks. She's always been so closed, and I wonder again at my middle child's strength and vulnerability. She equals her brothers in activity and energy, but her heart has always been different.

Elle reaches for the coffee pot, refilling our cups, and Jam returns to the kitchen for more coffee, gently resting his hands on her shoulders, which she instinctively cuddles into, as he sets more coffee down. There's a couple who are so well-suited together. They look like they've shared all their lives together, not just the last year. They have the ease of Cain and Lucy and Jason and Shelly, who have been together since secondary school, when Jason finally got around to asking out his friend to their end-of-school dinner. He came home with a stupid grin on his face that he still wears now when he looks to his wife. In just a few years they'll be looking at an empty nest, but they'll enjoy their time together just as Joe and I do. I imagine it helps that I have my crafting clubs, and he has his workshop to potter around. Maybe Jason and Shelly would like that holiday home in Cornwall they've mentioned a time or two?

Christmas Day Evening

Elle

I sink heavily into the sofa in the living room, opposite Lucy and Cain. Lottie is playing with one of her toys with Grandad. Nancy is the picture of happiness in the armchair.

'I don't think I've ever eaten so much food at one sitting - it was fabulous, Lucy - thank you!'

'Even I struggled.' Jam adds, walking into the room. He smiles at me, but doesn't sit next to me. He's gone again in a minute.

'That's a compliment if even hollow-legs Logan felt full, Luce.' Cain kisses her forehead and she snuggles into him, her fingers wrapped around her coffee and her man.

I love their Christmas tree, with their snow-tipped branches and traditional decorations. No longer surrounded by presents, a display of standing felted animals catch up on a snow-covered scene. I've had the most perfect day and I'm trying not to think of all the other Christmas Days I've missed out on. Although, I think, as Shelly and Jason join us, sitting on another sofa, next to their plugged-in pair of teenagers, being all together in Nashville is probably a very different experience to being all together on the wild Atlantic Ocean. Even I wouldn't be tempted to head out for a swim, and especially not after an eight course meal. Staying in this oversized log cabin in the woods feels just like how Christmas should be.

Jam is back again, with a tray of champagne glasses. I have no room in my stomach to even consider just licking the bubbles. My thoughts are said aloud by Lucy and Nancy, who are content with their coffee. Olivia looks up from her technical device, a look of interest in her eyes. A brief nod from her Mum and she lowers her headphones leaning forward, paying attention to the wider family.

Glasses are filled and passed around, and Joe steps back from playing with Lottie. Jam hands her a plastic glass of sparkling water and she walks slowly, with definite purpose, over to her Mum. So very grown up already.

When Jam reaches me, his eyes offer a thousand words as I take the glass, his fingers resting on mine for a moment.

'I think there's just one more present under the tree. For Elle.' He approaches a felted penguin, which is indeed holding a real parcel, about the size of a shoe box. I stand up and accept the beautifully wrapped box, carefully sliding the ribbon to one side and offering it to Lottie to play with. But instead of a pair of shoes, there's another, slightly smaller box. Then another.

Laughter escapes from around the room as we're taking in the different boxes, all wrapped beautifully in blue and silver paper, tied with white velvet ribbon. As my fingers release another package, a small, turquoise box falls into my hand.

'Wow.' Lucy gasps, before putting her cup to her lips. Jam moves the larger boxes away from me, as I open the final box. My heart loops as the most perfect ring stares at me. I look up to Jam, but he's now on the floor, one knee bent, his chocolate eyes level with mine.

Everyone else fades away as I look from Jam back to the ring, a curved white-gold band, encasing a stunning round diamond, flanked by two aquamarine pear shaped stones. I can only nod to his unasked question then suddenly the room erupts. Jam takes the ring from the box, places it on the fourth finger of my left hand. It fits perfectly.

'A toast. To the happiest day of my life. So far.' Jam says, and he places my glass back in my hand.

'To the no-longer elusive Mrs Jam' he whispers.

Then I'm in his arms and his lips are on mine, far, far too briefly.

Lucy is the first to wrap us in a hug, squealing, swiftly followed by Cain and then everyone else.

A roller coaster of happiness crashes through me, and I can't stop admiring the stunning declaration on my left hand.

'I wanted your ring to represent us' he says. 'The white-gold is from a pendant necklace of Mum's, reshaped to represent waves. The two ocean-coloured stones are us, in the water, and you Elle-Rawcliffe-soon-to-be-Logan-are a diamond of a woman.'

This time I kiss him deeply, my arms cradling either side of his head, holding my glass as upright as I possibly can.

As I pull away, his arms wrap tighter around my waist and I know I never want to let him go.

Then a thought dawns on me and I give him that look.

'What was with all the champagne, Logan? Pretty presumptuous of you to expect that I'd agree to be yours forever and ever?'

He groans just a fraction of what I'm going to elicit from him later on.

'I was pretty confident you'd be up for our next adventure together. And if you'd decided you weren't, I would have set the world record for downing ten glasses of Dom.'

Jam and I return to the sofa, our glasses topped up by Cain, and I know I have the daftest, widest grin on my face, because I suspect it's mirrored in Jam's face. Lucy and Shelly have lots of ideas about weddings, reminiscing about their own days. I half-listen, mostly distracted by the perfect ring now forever nestled on my left hand. My body moulds perfectly to Jam's, his arm draped around my shoulder. Every so often his fingers stray to that magic spot behind my ear and eventually my adrenalin gives way to a different kind of emotional need.

I fake-yawn, stretching my arms up dramatically and wiggling the fingers on my left hand.

'I have had the best Christmas Day in forever, Sis, but this ring is making me so very, very, tired. I think I have to go and lie it down.'

'I completely understand, Elle.' She grins, squashing me in a hug.

After a much longer goodbye than I'd anticipated, Jam and I were finally outside by ourselves.   We are definitely going to his place tonight.

Under a clear star-filled sky, he wraps his arms around me and kisses me like I'd needed him to all evening.

'Thank you for saying yes, Elle' he murmurs, brushing hair from my forehead.

I nod, unable to take my eyes from his.

'Thank you for coming to the airport for me' I whisper.

'I was going to propose on Boxing Day.'

I didn't think my knees could have weakened any more.

'But it was right, being surrounded by everyone, wasn't it?'

'Absolutely. I had no idea. But it was just perfect. The way you'd boxed the ring up, the actual ring, the moment I realised what was happening. I couldn't have planned it better.'

I grin.

We saunter back to Jam's house, the usual ten minutes taking hours it feels like.

Once at his house, he unlocks the front door and I follow in behind him, the enormity of our future together stretching out before me.

'I know you're not a fan of Nashville, Elle, so we can live in a different city. I can join Cain and Seb...'

I silence him with a soft kiss as we lean against his sofa.

'Nashville is where you are, and so I will be; we'll hit the oceans when we can.'

'All the chances we get, sweetheart. And we don't have to stay here, we can buy a new house, maybe nearer ... '

'This is the city where I first knew I loved you, and where you have just proposed. It's going to be the place we marry, as soon as we can. And, it's really not far from an airport at all.'

Epilogue

Lucy and Cain

As their cab journeys Lucy and Cain from JFK airport to midtown Manhattan, Cain can't stop looking at Lucy. He is more in love with his wife now than he was even half a decade ago, when they first visited New York. They have three whole days and two long nights just between them.

'I know what you're thinking, Cain.' Lucy says softly in his ear.

'You do?'

'Yes, and I will hungrily spend time in any hotel with you, ordinarily. But we're in New York City. For New Year's Eve.' She glances out of the window as the historical icons of the city flash by; they're nowhere near their midtown hotel yet. Her eyes revert back to her husband and best friend, his eyes mirroring the festive sparkle in her own eyes. They could be on the set of one of Lucy's favourite 80s films, perhaps Big or Cocktail. Perhaps Harry will meet Sally; they will definitely take Manhattan.

He laughs and kisses her slowly.

Lucy is glad she let Elle convince her to smooth and straighten her hair, which was finally looking healthy again after having Em.

'After we've – thoroughly - checked in to our hotel, it's dinner at The Top of the Rock, so I can see the whole of Manhattan. Then back to the room to change into our gladdest rags for the benefit concert at Carnegie Hall. Quick sleep, and then it's on to day two.'

As Lucy talks, Cain moves closer. The scent of the perfume he bought her for her last birthday surrounds him and one side of his mouth curls up even further into a smitten smile. This year he'll give her an early birthday present; the Art Deco blue sapphire, diamond and platinum necklace will perfectly compliment her navy cocktail dress as well as her eyes. He knows she won't run off when he presents the box to her before dinner.

'Tomorrow I'm so excited to visit as many museums as we can, stopping for coffee and deli sandwiches.'

'Then back to our hotel.'

Lucy stops running through the itinerary and smiles at the man always by her side. The cab slows down as their spa hotel approaches. They both glance out of the windows, their hands wrapped together.

After ticking off all the items off Lucy's list on their first day in New York they return to the hotel just before midnight.

'Wow, what a Christmas.' Lucy yawns, sinking down onto the queen-sized bed, navy material billowing out around her knees.

'Worth all of the lists?' Cain grins, taking off his boots and joining her on the bed, resting on his side, so he can see more of his wife. He loves how the necklace draws his attention.

'Absodefinitely. God, I still feel like I'm drunk on one of Bonnie's concoctions. Maybe we'll take lots of flights next year with Em until she gets used to them, then we can go to Cornwall next Christmas. I don't know how Nancy has done this every year. I'm shattered.'

'So you don't want to go out dancing later?' he asks, his fingers tracing her ribs.

'I did not say that.'

'And it's your birthday tomorrow.'

'Exactly. Still manages to sneak up on me. Still, I remember when New Year's Eve in New York City changed everything for me.'

Cain turned over onto his stomach, his head nestled in his hands.

'Not my finest hour.'

'Yeah, the upcoming month was horrendous. But.' Lucy manoeuvres her way underneath him, his hand reaches out to pull her closer. 'Sometimes we need an explosion to find the diamond. New York is when I knew I loved you. New York is a hotel room and a steak dinner overlooking the city, and catching my breath because I knew you loved me. Everything else got sorted out.'

'Promise me you'll always tell me how you're feeling? Even if you're feeling exhausted, or elated or angry or ...'

'Horny?' Lucy adds and Cain burrows his laugh in his happy place, in the crook of Lucy's neck.

'Everything.' He growls, sending ripples along her throat.

'Everything.' Lucy agrees.

Jam and Elle

Elle hasn't felt so happy in years, being surrounded by her family and new friends.

She has even flexed her style muscles, to preen her sister for her surprise break to New York. And, in familiarity if not blood, her sister-in-law Cassie, offering tips and advice for a New Year Party outfit. Elle enjoyed once again delving into cosmetics and brushes and blenders and hair straighteners - irons feels like something she should wield along an ironing board, and that's not her thing. She chose outfits and lead the way on presentation – it was like her treasured Canva graphics software had come to life.

Teen Olivia had sat in Lucy's bedroom watching proceedings, in a similar awe to the one Lottie had had most of Christmas towards her big cousin. Elle couldn't help but dish out advice on only choosing the best skincare you can afford, and not worrying about applying make up for hours for daily trips to school. Work with what nature intended and enhance, not replace.

As the last brush was tidied away and her subjects sailed off to their various New Year celebrations, she looked at herself in the mirror. Literally, being in love was her best feature right now, and she could see it shine from within. Any cheesier and she'd be producing a late night beauty infomercial, which she'd formed an obsession with lately, trying to guess the price of the products before it was revealed.

Elle, wearing her favourite turquoise dress, and Jam, dressed in a tuxedo, arrived at Bonnie's New Year's Eve party a little while after Cassie. As they entered the festive atmosphere, they saw Cassie and Bonnie heading upstairs, too far away to shout to and be heard.

They drank cocktails, played – and Elle won – drinking games, danced and finally managed to say hello to Bonnie and Cassie. By just after ten there was only one place they wanted to start their new year. An Uber was called and they headed back.

Early the next morning, in the living room, Elle stood in her robe, admiring the view of the woods through the glass wall.
'So, future Mrs Jam, when shall we go looking for a place of our own in Nashville?'

'Pardon?' Elle turned to face her fiancé. It would be a while before she tired of using that title. 'What's wrong with here?'

'Here?' Jam repeated.

'Yes, as in secluded, and just far away enough from family, at least until meal times.'

'Don't get me wrong, I will live anywhere with you, but I love this house, and would rather not move. But wouldn't it feel odd, not having chosen somewhere together?'

Elle stepped closer to him.

'Let me ask you this, Mr Jam, have you cleaned up after the hordes of women that have been through here?'

'No woman has ever been here, Elle.'

'Exactly. This is already our place.' She reached up onto tiptoes and kissed her fiancé until they forgot about interior decorations.

Nancy and Joe

Nancy snuggled up next to Joe in their king-sized at the writing retreat, surrounded by Christmas and another year of happy memories.

The kids were occupied, the grandkids were asleep. Time for a spot of TV host Graham Norton welcoming in the New Year in the UK.

Jason and Shelly had thought they were crazy retiring to bed so early, but they hadn't yet been married 30 years so still enjoyed later nights and later mornings. Jason had taken Shelly out for dinner date to the city. Spending more time together was imminent, as Ben and Olivia found more independence.

'Christmas in Nashville turned out okay, didn't it?' Joe asked rhetorically, as he bit into a cracker and Swiss cheese. He knew Nancy was smiling. He hadn't been married to his wife for three decades without knowing her. And he would always work hard to make her happy.

Nancy had loved watching Ben teach Lottie how to use a Kindle – with appropriate parental controls applied – to show her how to create basic animation. Lottie was a keen learner and doted on everything her big cousin Ben told her to do. Very different to the negotiation skills that Nancy had seen her employ with Lucy and Cain.

It had also been wonderful listening to the normally shy Olivia read stories to an enthralled Em. Her eldest granddaughter's desires for travel were beginning to show, as she expressed wishes that she could convince her parents to travel across the United States and maybe drop her off in Nashville. Nancy would mention her thoughts to Jason and Shelly, who took very little opportunity for travel. Their children would be leaving home in a few years – even earlier, Nancy suspected, for Olivia – and they would have to get used to living with each other again. Being a so-called empty-nester meant learning how to fall in love with your partner all over again, when you didn't have the crutch of a familiar routine to support you. Nancy and Joe had done it, though, and she was sure Jason and Shelly still held independent interests – Shelly with her books and Jason with his interest in technology – and their shared interests of cooking to understand and relate to each other.

Nancy had loved watching her family expand over the years, as first Lucy joined them, and then her sister, Elle, was welcomed in. She was a character all right, and would certainly keep Jam's heart. He had an uncle out in San Diego, California that she had met once in the summer. Nancy knew any friend of Cain's was always welcome in Cornwall, and that extended to his family, too.

And if truth be known, she had enjoyed being a guest at Christmas, not the host running around making sure everything ran smoothly. Lucy had done a fantastic job, maybe they could come back to Nashville next Christmas? Maybe even factor in a little shopping trip in Chicago beforehand, perhaps catch a show.

Yes, Christmas in Nashville would be a wonderful new tradition.

Cassie

I should never have let Elle loose on my hair and make-up.

I mean, I look good, but I don't look like me. This isn't who I am.

I didn't even know rose gold glitter eye shadow was a thing. Never mind primer and setter. I feel like one of Mum's feature walls. I press my lips together again, assured by Elle that even Jam has to work hard to dislodge the pigment. I have never bought fuchsia lipstick, but Elle had received the lipstick - sorry, matte lip lacquer - as part of a gift set. I was sure she'd applied the wand across my mouth to shush my protests.

Traffic has been light tonight, and I could see street lights ahead. According to my GPS we'd be arriving any minute. I tried to smooth down my dress, which was futile on gold glitter. I ran my hands through my voluminous hair, but the nerves and the palm perspiration were still present.

The Uber pulled up and before I could change my mind, the front door of the building opened up and the wood nymph I'd only known for ten days bolted towards the car.

We almost collided as I stepped onto the rocky ground.

'Cassie!' I'm so glad you could make it. You look incredible. I love me a party dress.' She shimmied her body in her twenties-inspired silver sequined dress, fringing brushing her thighs.

Bonnie wraps me up in an extended hug and I tried to keep my breath steady and not inhale her grapefruit scented shampoo.

Once inside the lively party she retrieves two whiskey-based cocktails from a passing tray, holding out one for me.

'Come on, let me show you around.'

I take the glass, sipping gladly. Bonnie slips her arm through mine and introduces me to everyone in Nashville it feels like.

I could only remember Bonnie.

As midnight approached I wandered purposefully outside to avoid the social pressure to be with someone at the turn of a new year. The cool air felt therapeutic against my skin and I gulped gratefully. This had been the best party I'd been to in a long time. I probably had been working quite hard this year. But the new school buildings would soon be finished, and then what?

'There you are.'

I turned around quickly at Bonnie's voice, remaining upright only by the fence suddenly behind me.

'Hey. It's a great party.'

'I get all my mixing skills from my sister.' She winks and steps forward, handing me a tumbler of clear liquid and ice. It was the clearest drink I'd seen all evening.

'Water.' She whispered in my ear. I tried to ignore the goosebumps raining down my arms. 'As midnight nears, I swap out every other drink with one of these.'

'Explains why your skin is so clear.' I blurted out. Like I'd been obsessing over her face all Christmas.

'Thanks.' she smiled, not unnerved by my awkwardness.

'Your skin is pretty awesome, too.'

I bring the glass to my mouth, unable to tear myself away from her violet eyes as I drink. Ice numbs my lips.

'Won't your family miss you to bring in the new year?' I said eventually.

She shook her head lightly.

'I like the view out here.'

I doubted all the *horchata* in Quito could quench my thirst.

Singing increased in volume in the house and the countdown began.

'I like you, Cassie.'

'Oh, yeah? It might be the water talking, but I like you, too.'

Her smile widens and we step even closer.

'Happy New Year, Cass.'

'Happy New Year, Bonnie.' I smile.

Her lips land on mine like a butterfly, their wings beating time throughout my body.

My phone then rings out a dance on the table beside us and we pull apart grinning.

I retrieve the message from Uber, annoyed with myself for booking an early ride home.

Bonnie traced her fingers rapidly along my arm, nestling her hand naturally in my left hand.

'Want to go back to my place?' she asks.

I nodded and we kiss like we mean it, teeth and senses colliding.

In the car I glance at my slightly smeared but smudge-free mouth in the mirror; Elle had been spot-on with the lip lacquer advice.

Acknowledgements

Dear reader, thank **you** for buying, or downloading, Everything This Christmas. I hope you loved spending time with Lucy, Elle, Nancy and Cassie as much as I enjoyed sharing their stories with you. Love is everything, and I love how my first romance series is growing; conversations I've had with you have helped to guide some of the storylines, and I have a host of other adventures lined up for the Lizard Guest House and Nashville Narrators!

Huge thanks to my fabulous friend and editor, Liz, who reads these stories with her acute eye far faster than I can amend the corrections.

These stories would take even longer to write if I didn't have the behind-the-scenes support of Pete and Eve, for the love and pride they share with me about writing, alongside their understanding of my need to write.

Thank you to my family for their vocal support of my stories, celebrating and sharing news of my books to absolutely anyone who stops still long enough to listen. Even if they just phone up to ask you about your energy supplier.

Thank you to everyone who comments on my social media posts, shares news and writes reviews about my books and pre-orders titles long before the final version is finished).

The *Love is Everything* series is available at your nearest Amazon.

Everything, Except You
Discover the long-distance love story of Lucy and Cain as they work out how to balance love with life, Nashville with London.

Everything and Nothing
Lucy's sister Elle has always had everything she's ever wanted. Except Cain's drummer, Jam. Who knew their love would take them from Thailand to Newquay, by way of Nashville?

Catch up with Cassie's story in Everything For Her, coming September 2021.
For the first time in her life Cassie isn't certain about her future. Can Lena help her find her way back to a self she hadn't dared dream was possible?

About the author

Emma Jordan has been writing creatively since she could first hold a pen. Many countries and adventures later she realised her obsessions with travel, country music – the perfect three minute stories – weren't going anywhere, so combined the tales with her love of romance to finally become a published fiction writer at the age of 42.

When she's trying to distract herself from writing she can be found on Twitter, Instagram and Facebook courtesy of her alter ego, dgtlwriter. The only thing Emma enjoys more than coffee and cake is chatting with readers - so feel free to say hello online.

Emma is currently working on a second romance series, as well as continuing with the **Love is Everything** stories, at least until the characters ask her to stop.

Printed in Great Britain
by Amazon